Ghost Years

Ghost Years

BARRY GIFFORD

SEVEN STORIES PRESS
New York • Oakland • London

SEVEN STORIES PRESS
140 Watts Street
New York, NY 10013
www.sevenstories.com

College professors and high school and middle school teachers
may order free examination copies of Seven Stories Press titles.
Visit https://www.sevenstories.com/pg/resources-academics
or email academic@sevenstories.com.

Library of Congress Cataloging-in-Publication Data

Names: Gifford, Barry, 1946- author.
Title: Ghost years / Barry Gifford.
Description: New York : Seven Stories Press, 2024.
Identifiers: LCCN 2024003414 | ISBN 9781644213773 (trade paperback) | ISBN
   9781644213780 (ebook)
Subjects: LCGFT: Short stories.
Classification: LCC PS3557.I283 G56 2024 | DDC 813/.54--dc23/eng/20240126
LC record available at https://lccn.loc.gov/2024003414

ACKNOWLEDGMENTS

"Pops" and "Castor and Pollux in America" originally appeared in *Southwest Review*
(Dallas); "Another Irishman" originally appeared in *Narrative* (San Francisco); and "Big
Hands" originally appeared in the *Santa Monica Review*.

Drawings on pages 179 and 180 by Scott Gillis. All other drawings by Barry Gifford.

This book is for Jimbo

"Each artist seems . . . to be the
native of an unknown country, which
he himself has forgotten . . ."
—Marcel Proust, The Captive

"The hand that wounded you
shall also heal."
—Claudius, Emperor of Rome,
quoting from the tale of
Telephus and Achilles

"nothing counts save the quality of the
affection"
—Ezra Pound, Canto LXXVII

CONTENTS

AUTHOR'S NOTE

This book is about the "ghost years, that time in your life you don't know won't never come again," as Mrs. Cunningham tells Roy and her son, Tommy, in "Ghost Years." Almost all of *Ghost Years* takes place in the 1950s. No doubt in the present day certain points of view taken by various characters as well as some of the language will be considered politically incorrect, even racist or sexist, by discerning readers. This is part of the verisimilitude, it's intentional. That's the way it was.

—B.G.

ROY'S CHRONOLOGY

Secrets of An Actress

Kitty's friend May June, whom Kitty had met before her son Roy was born, when both women were hat and glove models in New York, was an actress who had recently suffered a nervous breakdown. May had come to Chicago, where her mother and sister and Kitty lived, to rest and recover. She was living in Hollywood at the time of her collapse, following a bad divorce and forced withdrawal from the movie she was working on.

Kitty and May were the same age, twenty-eight. They had kept in touch by correspondence and occasionally by telephone during the six years since Kitty had gotten married and moved to Chicago. Now separated from her own husband, Kitty kept busy raising her son, who was five years old, and working part-time modelling fur coats at the Merchandise Mart.

May was staying with her unmarried sister, Mona, who worked as a registered nurse at Edgewater Beach Hospital, where May was being treated for her unstable condition. It wasn't until almost a month after her arrival in Chicago that she felt well enough to meet Kitty for lunch at Armando's Restaurant, which was next door to Kitty's husband Rudy's liquor store and pharmacy.

"Kitty, can Rudy give me some pills?"

"Don't you get medication from the hospital?"

"Yes, but they're not enough. I need something stronger."

Both women were drinking martinis and May was chain-smoking Lucky Strikes.

"Are you allowed to drink alcohol while you're on medication?" asked Kitty.

May exhaled a cloud of smoke before saying, "My doctor asked me what I like to drink. I told him gin martinis, very dry, and he said to limit myself to one."

May quickly polished off the martini she had in hand, held up her glass and signalled to their waiter.

"May, you just said that your doctor limited you to one."

"I took it to mean one at a time."

Kitty took a sip from her glass, then said, "I'm sure Rudy won't give you anything while you're under a doctor's care. He could lose his pharmacist's license."

May's second martini arrived. She stubbed out her cigarette and lit another.

"Did something bad happen to you in Hollywood?"

"Too many things. After I got fired from *Don't Say No*, I was broke and lonely, drinking too much, not thinking straight. I made a few regrettable decisions. More than a few."

May picked up her glass, looked into it as if it were a crystal ball, then put it down.

"I turned some tricks. Slept with guys who'd been after me, not really strangers, but men I never would have gone with had I not been desperate and friendless."

"Surely you have friends there, people who could have helped you out."

"I was humiliated. I didn't want to beg. It was an easy way to get money."

"Begging would have been better than prostituting yourself."

"Every girl out there prostitutes herself one way or another, most often by marrying men they don't love."

May lifted her glass again and drank a little.

"You're right, Kitty, I won't ask Rudy, or bug you to."

"Trust your doctor, May. Mona knows who's best at Edgewater. And just rest, you'll get better."

May smiled for the first time since she'd been with Kitty. Her eyes were bloodshot and her cheeks were pale. Hollywood had fled from her face.

"I was sorry to hear about you and Rudy separating. Any chance you'll get back together?"

"I don't think so. We're friends, good friends, and he's very good to Roy. Also generous. I'm going through with the divorce. What happened to Bob?"

"He blamed me for walking out on him. Told the judge I'd made a play for a rich producer friend of his."

"Did you?"

"I don't really know. I might have. Whatever I did, it wasn't serious. And Bob had his peccadillos, some I knew about, some I didn't."

Kitty laughed. "That's a good word for it. Everyone has their secrets."

"In Hollywood somebody always has the goods on you and uses it sooner or later. I'm so glad you didn't follow me there. Rudy will always be your friend, and you have Roy."

Their waiter came over.

"Are you ladies ready to order lunch? The kitchen closes in fifteen minutes."

"What's your name?" May asked him.

"Roberto."

"You have lovely, wavy hair, Roberto," said May. "Do you dye it?"

"We aren't staying," Kitty told him. "Bring me the check."

He walked away.

May lit another Lucky Strike off of her half-smoked one. She tossed back her head and her hair fell over one eye like Rita Hayworth's did in *Gilda*.

"Do you remember in *Streetcar Named Desire* when Stanley Kowalski is terrorizing his shaky sister-in-law and shouts in her face, 'Ha, ha, ha, Blanche!' That's what I say to myself after I realize I've done something terrible. I'm not Blanche DuBois,

I'm a beast. There's no forgiveness in me, Kitty, at least not for myself."

May's hand holding the cigarette was trembling. She tried to put it to her lips but couldn't find them.

"Come on, May, I'll drive you back to Mona's."

"My secret is that I don't have one. I can't keep anything to myself. Or is it from myself?"

Roberto came back.

"There's no charge for the drinks," he said.

"Bring me another," said May.

May June

Worrying About the Weather

The first thing Roy's mother, Kitty, read in the *Tribune* every morning was the weather report. After that she read Jenny Knight's gossip column, *Knight Out*. Most of the time that's all she read in the newspaper.

"Mom, why do you only read about the weather?"

"I read Jenny Knight, too. The rest isn't worth bothering with. If the sky's going to fall or already has there's nothing we can do about it. I can't control whatever else happens."

"You can't control the weather, either."

"No, but I can prepare myself for it. Not yesterday's, of course, but today's and tomorrow's."

The only part of the paper Roy looked at was the comic strip page. He didn't understand all of them but he liked the different ways the characters looked and how animals spoke like people.

"If the newspaper says it's going to be a stormy day do you get worried?"

"No. Well, sometimes. It depends on what my plans are, if the weather will affect them. Here in Chicago the weather can change in a hurry. When we're in Key West it's not the same, we have more time to get ready."

"Would you rather be in a hurricane or a blizzard?"

"Oh, definitely not a hurricane, it lasts too long. Sometimes the sky sits on top of you for days and the rain doesn't stop, it makes me crazy."

"It can snow for days, too."

"I like the snow on the first day, maybe even the second. After that it gets dirty and it's hard to get around, to drive or even walk. A hurricane can make you feel like it's the end of the world."

"Is it possible for the world to end?"

Kitty got up from her chair at the kitchen table.

"I'm going to make coffee for myself. Do you want cereal? We have Raisin Bran and Cheerios. Or I can make oatmeal."

"Raisin Bran with a banana cut up in it. Dad said he liked when it snowed a lot because it reminded him of being in the old country. He told me the Gypsies put hats with large brims on their horses' heads to keep snow out of their eyes when they have to pull carts and wagons around the villages. They cut holes in the hats so the horses' ears could poke through."

"Sometimes I think your father would have preferred to stay in Bucovina with the Gypsies rather than go with his family to America."

"How old was he when they left the old country?"

"Ten, four years older than you are now."

"What language do the Gypsies speak?"

"Romany, I think it's called."

"How come Dad never spoke it?"

"Who could understand him if he did? He probably forgot most of it."

"Did he teach you any words?"

Kitty laughed. "Dja devlesa! Goodbye! That's all I can remember."

"Dja devlesa!" said Roy.

"Look out the window, honey, it's really coming down."

"If Dad were alive I'd ask him how to say it's raining in Gypsy."

Plouă (It's raining.)

744 North Rush Street

"Where's your pay phone?"

"Haven't got one."

"Every place got one."

"Not this place. There's one across the street in Tony Zale's restaurant."

"Tony Zale? I remember when he decked Baby Kid Chocolate, fourth round. He won the title after that. Man of steel, hardest punchin' middleweight I ever seen. He's from Gary, you know. I'm from Whiting, steel towns."

"Tony's usually around this time of day. Stop in and say hello to him."

"I'll bet he's got a phone in the bar."

The man left Rudy's liquor store.

"Who was that guy, Dad?" asked Roy.

"Guy lookin' for a phone."

"You've got lots of phones in the basement."

"Those are private lines, Roy. Not for customers."

Rudy and Roy, who was seven and a half years old, were standing together in the doorway to Lake Shore Liquors on the corner of Chicago Avenue and Rush Street. It was almost noon on a Saturday in October. The store wasn't busy. Most of the people who resided and/or worked in the nightclub district weren't even awake yet. Lake Shore Liquors stayed open twenty-four hours.

"Dad?"

"Yes, son?"

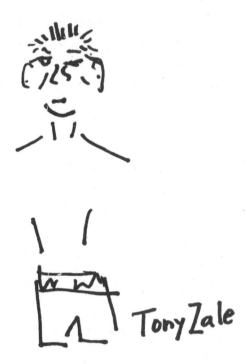

Tony Zale

"Are you ever afraid someone'll come in with a gun and rob the store?"

"There are too many cops comin' in and goin' out. Nobody from around here would try it."

"What about a stranger? Somebody not from this neighborhood."

"That's only happened once, on a weekday night, ten o'clock."

"Did he get the money?"

"No, Eddie shot him. One in each leg from behind. The guy never saw him. Lou was at the register with a .38 pointed at him."

"He must have been scared."

"You know your Uncle Lou, he doesn't spook easy."

"Maybe because he was in the war. He told me he shot a lot of Krauts."

"Eddie got the guy before he could fire a shot. Lou called the cops."

"When Tony Zale let me try on the gloves he used when he knocked out Rocky Graziano I asked him if Rocky scared him."

"What did he say?"

"He said Rocky threw punches even when he was falling down. Tony was afraid he'd get hit below the belt."

"Those boys fought each other three times, they know every trick in the book. Rocky could land one accidentally on purpose."

Roy laughed. "That's funny, Dad. How could something be an accident if someone did it on purpose?"

"You'll find out."

A hard wind was blowing debris in from the street.

"Come inside," Rudy said, and closed the door.

A No Good Kid

When Eddie Metz was thirteen years old he set fire to a bum sleeping in an alley. The bum was passed out drunk on cheap wine or whiskey. At nine o'clock one night Metz bought a gallon of gas for twenty-one cents at the Mohawk station on the corner of Ojibway and Rockwell, carried it in a plastic kids' pail he'd found in a sandbox at a park playground and went in search of a bum to burn. He found him collapsed in the weeds of an empty lot on the fringe of an alley between Mohican and Laramie streets, poured the gas on the guy over his legs and up to his neck, tossed the pail into the weeds, then took out a book of matches from a coat pocket, struck several of them and ignited the gas. Eddie backed away and watched the flames engulf the bum's body before running down the alley. He was never caught and he never knew if his victim had died or not. Eddie didn't care, he'd done what he wanted to do.

Roy and his friends in the neighborhood, all of whom were nine, ten and eleven years old, knew who Eddie Metz was and they didn't mess with him. He supposedly attended Stambolov Vocational, a school for retarded and so-called problem boys whose behavior was considered unfit for public or parochial schools. Stambolov was named for a Bulgarian statesman of the previous century who had sponsored a law separating inferior and unruly children from their families and banished them to labor camps until the age of eighteen, at which time the boys were conscripted into the Bulgarian army and the girls forced to work as street cleaners. Eddie and the other throwaways from Chicago schools called Stambolov "Stumblebum" prep. They knew their next misstep would cause them to be sent either to a state reformatory or, if they were at least sixteen, to the men's prison in Joliet, Illinois.

Roy had only one personal encounter with Eddie Metz. On a morning before school Roy went into Kapp's sandwich shop and school supplies store across the street from Torquemada Elementary to buy some pencils and found Eddie arguing with the owner, Wilbur Kapp, about the price of a powdered doughnut.

"It's a dime, Eddie," said Kapp. "I told you."

"It ain't worth more than a nickel. Come on, Kapp, I got a nickel right here."

Metz took a coin out of a pocket and put it on the counter.

"Look, an Indian head."

"Not enough, Eddie."

"Hey, you," Eddie said to Roy, "you got five cents I can borrow? I'll pay you back."

"I have fifteen cents. I need twelve to buy three pencils."

"Okay, gimme three cents, that'll make eight. Kapp, I can give you eight, how's that? The kid'll give you fifteen to cover his pencils plus what I owe."

Kapp handed Eddie the doughnut, who took it and walked out without saying anything more. Roy showed three pencils to Kapp and put a dime and a nickel on the counter. Kapp scooped them up, deposited them in his cash register, and handed three pennies to Roy.

"Take your change, Roy. Forget about Metz, he's a no good kid."

Whenever Roy saw Eddie on the street after that he kept his distance. Metz never spoke to him about the three cents or anything else, and a year or so later he disappeared from the neighborhood. An eighth grader named Doug Groot who'd hung around with Metz before being arrested for stealing bicycles and sent to

Stambolov Vocational for two months, told police that Metz had bragged to him about having torched a sleeping bum. This claim could not be proved and Eddie was gone, so nothing came of it.

What Roy and the others never knew was that many years later, when Eddie Metz learned of a festival held in the Nevada desert called Burning Man, at the conclusion of which a large wooden figure of a man was set afire, he laughed out loud and shook his head. Eddie was seated on a stool at the Golden Gopher Bar on 8th Street in downtown Los Angeles when he heard this coming from the television set above the bar. A patron sitting a couple of stools away asked him what was so funny and Eddie said, "Those drugged up punks don't know what the real thing feels like."

"And you do?"

Eddie didn't answer right away, so the man asked him, "Were you in the war?"

Eddie took a swig of his double shot of Murphy's and said, "I've been at war since I was a kid."

Eddie Metz

Ghost Years

"You remember that guy Mickey Mikalski, used to hang out with Nick DeSantis?"

"Had a split lip."

"Hare lip. Had an operation to fix it. He's been tryin' to grow a mustache to cover up the scar but hair won't grow there."

"What about him?"

"He got nabbed boostin' a car. Drove it through a fence, how the cops caught him. Winky Wicklow says his Uncle Bob, who's a cop, thinks Mikalski'll get five years at Joliet 'cause he ain't a minor no more."

"That's rough."

"You know what the Arabs do to a horse thief?"

"What?"

"Cut off one of his hands so he has to eat and wipe his ass with the same hand."

"Who told you that?"

"My dad. He heard about it when he was in Morocco."

"Are he and your mother back together?"

"Sort of. He's been travelling a lot lately."

Roy and his friend Tommy Cunningham were sitting on the front steps of Tommy's house on a Saturday morning.

"It's gonna rain," said Tommy. "I don't think we'll get to play the game this afternoon. Which would you choose, Roy, five years in prison or lose a hand?"

"Be tough to play ball one-handed."

Tommy nodded. "I'd rather have a car than a horse."

"What's that about a horse?"

Tommy's mother stepped out of the house onto the front porch.

"Morning, Ma. I just told Roy I'd rather have a car to ride around in than a horse."

"Good morning, Mrs. Cunningham," said Roy.

"I liked to ride horses back in Ireland when I was a girl."

"Gee, Ma, you never told me that before."

"It was a long time ago, in my ghost years, that time in your life you don't know won't never come again. I remember my favorite, Princesa. She had Spanish blood, belonged to a farmer down the road from us. He let me ride her after school and on Sundays after church."

"Not on Saturdays?"

"Saturdays were for marketing and chores. Now it's every day and it's only police who ride horses in Chicago. What're you fellas up to?"

"We're supposed to play a ballgame against Margaret Mary's at Heart-of-Jesus, but looks like we'll be rained out."

"I could use a hand with the laundry."

Roy stood up.

"I'll see you at the park, Tommy, if it clears up. Bye, Mrs. Cunningham."

On his way home Roy thought about what Tommy's mother might have been like as a country girl in Ireland before her family moved to Chicago. She was a strong, heavyset woman now, with bright blue eyes and thick red hair. Her face had deep creases on the cheeks. Roy's mother, who was a few years younger than Mrs. Cunningham, had no lines on her face and she was much slimmer, but she was always nervous and worried about something. Mrs. Cunningham always seemed calm and spoke in a gentle way to Tommy and his brother Colin. Maybe his mother would be calmer if she had spent her childhood in the country and had a horse to ride instead of living in a big city and then being sent away to boarding school.

The sun was trying to break through the clouds. Roy decided to get his glove and go to the park even if it started to rain. On his way there he spotted a powder blue Cadillac getting gas at the Mohawk station across Ojibway Avenue. His mother was sitting in the front passenger seat next to a man Roy did not recognize. The man was wearing a brown Fedora and a beige trenchcoat, the kind private investigators wore in the movies. He was talking to Roy's mother and she was looking out the closed window on her side. Roy watched her for a minute until the attendant stopped pumping gas. The driver paid him, started the car and pulled out of the station. Roy's mother kept staring through her window.

His baseball cap was wet and water was leaking through into his hair but Roy began walking again toward the park. He was certain his mother had not seen him.

At the park six blue-and-whites were parked at a variety of angles in the street in front of the entrance Roy commonly used. A few people were gathered on the sidewalk in front of a line of several policemen who were blocking the way.

"What's going on?" Roy asked a man wearing a Cubs hat and a green tanker jacket.

"There's a dead body lyin' on the pitcher's mound. A kid, someone said."

"Did you hear the kid's name?"

"No. The cops aren't givin' out any information. They might not know yet."

Tommy Cunningham punched Roy in his left arm.

"All these people here to watch our game?"

"Thought you were helpin' your mother with the laundry."

"I did. Somebody get shot?"

"Maybe. There's a dead kid on the mound."

"You're jokin'. Who told you that?"

"Guy over there. Cops won't let anyone into the park."

"Let's go around to Kavanagh's house and go in through his backyard."

The boys ran around the block, cut through Terry Kavanagh's yard into the alley and crept up a dirt path where there weren't any cops. A bunch of men were standing around the infield, a couple of whom were taking photos. Tommy and Roy kept their distance and half hid behind a large Dutch elm tree. An ambulance drove into the park and stopped next to the first base foul line. Two male attendants wearing white coats and trousers jumped out, opened up the back doors of the ambulance and pulled out a stretcher. The men on the infield parted to let them through but not enough so that Roy and Tommy could see the body on the mound. It was ten minutes before the attendants carried out the stretcher. The corpse was covered with a white sheet but as it was being loaded into the ambulance the stretcher tilted and the sheet slipped off the face.

"It's Louie Fortini," said Tommy, "Artie Fortini's older brother. Remember him? He must be about twenty years old. He was a pitcher, had a tryout with the Braves but didn't get signed."

"You sure?"

"Yeah. He and Artie both got big hook noses. It's Louie for sure."

The ambulance drove out of the park the way it came in. Rain fell harder and some of the men walked off the infield.

"I wonder if his family knows," said Roy.

"The cops probably called them. They'll have to identify the body."

There was a flash of lightning followed by thunder.

"Let's get away from this tree," Roy said.

The next day there was an article in the *Sun-Times* about the dead boy. Louie Fortini had shot himself in the head with his father's gun, a Luger Anthony Fortini had taken off a fallen German soldier during the war and kept as a souvenir. Louie had been a day shy of his twenty-first birthday. In the article his father was quoted as saying that his son had been depressed ever since his unsuccessful tryouts for major league baseball teams.

On their way to school Tommy said to Roy, "I wonder if he tried out for the Cubs. He could throw a screwball. I saw him throw it in high school."

"Artie would know."

"Man, I'd never kill myself. What about you, Roy?"

Roy remembered his mother once saying that if things got any worse she'd commit suicide.

Before he could answer, Tommy said, "Do you think Louie told Artie he was thinking about shooting himself?"

"We shouldn't ask him that," said Roy.

Mrs. Cunningham

At Ciro's

"Kitty, you never told me you were in the movies!"

"Don't be silly, June. I only did a screen test when Rudy and I were in Hollywood on our honeymoon."

"Was it for a particular movie?"

"Sort of. Otto Feldman, an executive producer at RKO, was one of the people having dinner with us one night at Ciro's and he suggested I take a test for the role of Gene Tierney's younger sister in a picture to be called *Temperatures Rising* or *Raising the Temperature*, something like that. I don't think it ever got made."

"What was the test like? Did you say any lines?"

"Yes, one. They asked me to say, 'How do you know he won't let you?' I repeated it a couple of times, once looking directly into the camera, once while in my left profile."

"What did Rudy think about it?"

"He told me to go ahead, have fun."

Kitty and June DeLisa were sitting on a couch in the living room of Kitty's house in Chicago. June was waiting for her friend Kenny to pick her up to go for an early dinner.

"Are you sure you won't come with us? Bring Roy along, Kenny won't mind."

"I can't. Roy's been sleeping all afternoon. I think he's coming down with something."

A car honked in front of the house. June and Kitty both stood up.

"There's Kenny now. I want to hear more about your time in Hollywood."

"There's no more to tell. I never heard back from Mr. Feldman."

Otto Feldman

"Too bad. I bet you'd have been good. You were as pretty as Gene Tierney. Prettier."

"Stop it, June. You and Kenny have a good time. Where is he taking you?"

"The Danube, in the Churchill Hotel."

"Oh, I love their Chicken Kiev."

June kissed Kitty on her right cheek and ran out.

After she was gone, Kitty sat down again. She thought about Hollywood when she and Rudy had been there ten years before. No, eleven. She was twenty-one then. A snapshot, that's all. Like everything. Her mother gone, Rudy gone. Gene Tierney wasn't a big star anymore, not like she'd been in *Laura* when she was twenty-three. No other girl in Hollywood was prettier than she was, except maybe Hedy Lamarr.

Roy walked into the living room, rubbing his eyes. He climbed up onto the couch and put his head down in Kitty's lap. Kitty felt his forehead. It was cool. Rudy had left their table at Ciro's to make a phone call when Otto Feldman asked her if she liked being married. At the time, she hadn't understood what he meant.

Lake Superior

"Nappy Buchinsky's body turned up in Lake Superior, snagged in a trawler's fishing net a couple weeks ago. Took a while before he could be identified."

"In Michigan or Wisconsin?"

"Minnesota. His corpse is still in Duluth."

"Who told you?"

"Lefty's ex-brother-in-law, Max Milano."

Rudy Winston and his seven-year-old son, Roy, were sitting in the front seat of Rudy's idling Cadillac parked on Chicago Avenue in front of Rudy's store, Lake Shore Liquors and Pharmacy, listening to Phil Moore, a plainclothes cop, who was leaning on the driver's side door. Roy's father spoke to him through the open window.

"I was up there once," said Rudy, "last October, around the same time as now. It was already cold."

He rolled up the window and pulled the Caddy out into traffic.

"Dad, was Nappy Buchinsky a friend of yours?"

"I knew the guy. He came into the store once in a while."

"How do you think he wound up in the lake? Was he a fisherman?"

"Nappy Buchinsky's not worth thinking about, son."

"It's a mystery, though, huh?"

Rudy drove north on a bridge across the Chicago River.

"Not really. He could as easily ended up in the drink here."

Roy wanted to ask his father why he had been at Lake Superior the year before. As the Cadillac passed the *Tribune* building snow flurries began to hit the windshield but they didn't stick.

Twenty years later, Roy was on the western shore of Lake Superior. He remembered that Nappy Buchinsky's body was discovered there in a fishing net and his father telling him that he was not worth thinking about. Rudy had been dead for almost as long as Nappy. Thick fog hung over the lake so Roy could not see if there were any trawlers on it.

Nappy Buchinsky

ADW

"Winky's cousin Bonnie got arrested for tryin' to stab her teacher, Mrs. Rasmussen, with a knitting needle. Cops charged her for ADW."

"What's that?" Roy asked Jimmy.

"Assault with a deadly weapon."

"She's a seventh grader, isn't she? Why'd she do it?"

"Winky says Bonnie told her parents Mrs. Rasmussen threatened to flunk her if she didn't stop interrupting the class talkin' to her friends and talkin' back to her usin' bad words."

Jimmy Boyle lived next door to the Wicklows. He and Roy were both in fifth grade, Winky was in sixth. They were on the playground at Torquemada Grammar School waiting for the eight-forty bell to ring.

"Bonnie's big," said Roy, "bigger than Mrs. Rasmussen. Taller, anyway."

Jimmy pointed at a group of girls.

"There's Wendy, Winky's sister. Let's ask her what's happening."

Wendy was an eighth grader. Roy thought she was the prettiest girl in the school. He liked her long, honey-blonde hair that hung halfway down her back.

"Bonnie's in detention at juvey," Wendy told them. "She has to stay there until the hearing."

"When will that be?"

"Soon, I guess. My mother brought some sandwiches there for her yesterday but the cops wouldn't let Bonnie have them."

The bell rang. Wendy walked toward the school building. Roy stared at her hair.

"They could have charged Bonnie with attempted murder," he said.

"They don't put kids in the electric chair in Illinois," said Jimmy, "especially girls."

Wendy had disappeared.

When Roy got home in the afternoon his mother's husband, her third, Spanky Wankovsky, was sitting by himself in the living room drinking from a can of beer and smoking a cigarette, listening to a record on the phonograph. He was a jazz drummer who worked mostly at nights. Roy didn't like him but he often liked the records he played. Roy stood in the front hallway for a minute.

"Who's that?" he asked. "On the saxophone."

"Sonny Stitt, 'Autumn in New York.' How was school?"

"A girl I know might have to go to prison for trying to stab a teacher."

Wendy Wicklow

Spanky took a long drag on his cigarette and blew a couple of smoke rings.

"I didn't do good at school," he said, "but I was in the band. You and your pals should chip in and buy her a radio so she can listen to music in her cell."

Roy thought that was a good suggestion, but he doubted that Bonnie would be allowed to have it since she didn't even get to eat Jimmy's mother's sandwiches.

Anything

"Don't sweat it, I can get around anything."

"This ain't just anything."

Roy overheard this exchange between two men he'd never seen before while he was sitting at the lunch counter in his father's pharmacy and liquor store. Big Louise worked the counter, making and serving sandwiches and drinks. It was three o'clock on a Saturday afternoon in June. Roy, who was six and a half years old, was out of school for the summer. He liked to sit at the counter and talk to the customers, mostly single men and women who smoked cigarettes and nursed cups of coffee. He was waiting for Angelo, the organ grinder, and his monkey, Dopo, who performed on street corners in Chicago's nightclub district. Angelo played a portable organ while Dopo danced and collected change from passersby in his fez. They usually took a break around three-thirty and came into the drugstore and sat at the counter. Dopo would dunk a doughnut into his cup of coffee and share it with Roy. The two strangers whose conversation Roy had been listening to were sitting at the far end of the counter near the front door, which was kept open when, like today, the weather was good.

Roy's father, Rudy, came over and tickled Dopo under his chin, causing the monkey to chatter.

"He likes you, Dad."

"It's why he laugh," said Angelo.

"Dopo is a good customer," said Rudy.

"And a big tipper," said Big Louise, as she refilled Dopo's cup.

"What's a filthy ape doin' sittin' at a lunch counter?" said one of the men in the corner.

Dopo tipped his fez to Big Louise and showed his teeth. Rudy walked over to the man who had spoken.

"Finish your coffee and go," he said. "No charge, Louise."

Both of the men stared at Rudy for a moment, then stood up. Dopo made a screeching sound like a train putting on its brakes.

"Dopo say don't forget to leave tip," said Angelo.

One of the men reached into his pants pocket, took out a half dollar and slapped it down on the countertop before they left.

"I hope those guys don't come back," said Roy.

A couple of weeks later, Rudy asked Roy if he remembered the two men.

"Un huh. One of 'em insulted Dopo."

"He's in jail, the other one's dead."

"The guy who's dead said he could get around anything. The guy who's in jail didn't think he could."

"You can save yourself a lot of trouble, son, just by listening to what people say."

"Monkeys listen too, Dad."

Roy asked Big Louise if she knew what the crime was that the two men had committed.

"A hold up, Lou said. Nothin' big, a pawn shop maybe. Those Jews carry guns."

"What Jews?"

"Pawn brokers, most of 'em. I knew one, Max Fang, had a shop up on Congress, kept his big bills in an egg beater. Every so often a junkie came in shakin' a rod and cleaned out the register, in which Max had only ones and fives. The Jews are shrewd, Roy, they're survivors, had to be chased around like they been. My people are Polish Catholic and my grandfather used to say, 'If only I were a Jew I'd be a rich man.'"

"My dad is Jewish," said Roy, "so is Lou."

"Yeah, but they're different. Your dad is a tough guy but he's real generous when he wants to be, doesn't expect anything back. He knows how to take care of people. You could do worse than to be like him."

When his mother picked him up from the store later that afternoon, Roy told her about the two men and what Big Louise had said about his father and the Jews. Like Louise, his mother was a Catholic.

"Louise is right about your dad," she said, "but I can't say anything about the rest of the Jews."

Big Louise

Chicago 1956

Kitty had always gotten along well with her father-in-law, Ahab. He was fifty years older than Kitty when she married his youngest son, Rudy. Ahab loved to have Kitty on his arm when she accompanied him to a restaurant or nightclub. He had emigrated to America from Bucovina in the year following World War I with his four sons, his wife having died of tuberculosis during the war.

"In the Old Testament it says that Ahab fathered seventy boys," he told Kitty. "I believe had Bella lived the long life that she deserved we might have come close to his mark."

Ahab laughed after he said this, but it was clear to Kitty that even in his early seventies he remained strong and vigorous. The old man had remarried once, a year after coming to Chicago, where his uncle Ike had lived since before the war; unfortunately, Natalia died two years later in childbirth, as did their baby, a boy. Ahab decided never to marry again, to leave it to his sons to perpetuate the line. To his displeasure, however, his oldest son, David, fathered two daughters and his middle sons, Moses and Jerome, had not married. It was up to Kitty, Ahab told her, to give him a grandson, which she promptly did, naming him Roy— king—endearing Rudy's bride to him for the remainder of his life.

One Sunday afternoon in May, Kitty, Rudy and his father went together to Riverview, an amusement park on Chicago's north side. Kitty and Rudy rode a couple of the gentler roller coasters and competed at trying to knock down three milk bottles with a baseball, which neither of them managed to do. The three of them posed for a photograph together sitting inside a cardboard half moon, Kitty between the two men. In the photograph she looked even younger than her twenty-one years, and both Rudy and Ahab appeared relaxed and smiling.

Their outing was nearing an end as they were passing The Bobs, the fastest roller coaster in the park, when a man stood up at the apex of the climb to the top and leapt from the open car in which he, presumably, had been seated. Many people in the crowd screamed or shouted as they watched the man plunge to his death. A tall man standing next to Kitty said, "Happens about twice a year." Rudy grabbed Kitty's left arm and Ahab by his right and hurried them toward the exit.

That night Kitty said to Rudy, "I can't get the sight of that guy jumping off the roller coaster out of my mind. I still don't believe it really happened."

"When I was eight years old, before we left the old country, I saw a kid fall off the roof of an apartment building and hit the sidewalk in front of me. He must have been eleven or twelve, I didn't know him. He landed on his head and both of his eyes popped out."

"Rudy, stop! Don't tell me any more. You must have been horrified and frightened."

"Surprised, sure, but not frightened. I figured some other kid had pushed him over the edge."

"Did you tell your parents?"

"I don't remember. I don't think so."

"I hope I won't have a nightmare," Kitty said. "I'll never go to Riverview again. And you know that photo of us in the moon? If I look at it I'll always remember what happened."

"It's a nice picture," said Rudy, "let's keep it, anyway."

Parris Island

"I spent the summer I was sixteen on Parris Island, South Carolina, where my brother, Buck, was stationed with the navy. Our mother was married then to her second husband and they didn't want me around. I left boarding school and two days later I was put on a train at Union Station in Chicago. Buck was married to his first wife, Katarina, and since he was already a commissioned officer—a lieutenant commander—they had a nice apartment off the base.

"Katarina was a party giver, she liked to entertain, to have company. They even had a grand piano in the living room, which she encouraged me to play during their cocktail gatherings. Popular songs, 'Stardust,' 'You Stepped Out of a Dream,' 'Stars Fell on Alabama.' I was pretty good, I'd taken lessons since I was five, and my mother could play and sing. Most of the guests were officers and their wives, many of whom complimented me, and after they'd had a couple of Buck's martinis one or more of the men made suggestive remarks to me. Katarina protected me, though. She was very smart, she'd taught calculus and read poetry by Ezra Pound and T.S. Eliot. She was lousy elegant, sophisticated but unpretentious, she kept control of the scene. I liked her and admired her looks. She was a natural platinum blonde, a bit severe looking but attractive. She wore her hair pulled back tightly against her skull, which exaggerated her high ckeekbones and wide mouth. My brother was at his handsomest, he resembled Errol Flynn or Ronald Colman. The wives of the other officers were crazy for him. To her credit, Katarina got a kick out of their sometimes shameless behavior. She made sure these women knew he was her property and she revelled in their envy. I was quite shy at that time. I was impressed by Katarina's casually icy savoir-faire. Being in that atmosphere was a treat for me after having spent several months at Our Lady of Everlasting Obedience. I had a good time that summer on Parris Island."

"My, Kitty," said Polly Page, "it's fun to hear you talk about yourself. Are you this forthcoming when you see your psychiatrist?"

"Oh, no. I only saw him a couple of times. He prescribed pills that made me dopey. June DeLisa sent me to him, she lives on those pills. There was no way I could open up to him. I can't talk to men, I never could."

"Even your husbands?"

"Especially them. I tell stories about my life to Roy, he's a good listener."

"He's only eight years old, Kitty. He's incapable of understanding your innermost feelings about things, you can't share your most intimate thoughts."

Kitty lit a cigarette and looked out the dining-room window. Daylight was disappearing.

"Buck went to prison for two years. Did you know that?"

"No. What for?"

"While he was in the navy, as a civil engineer he was in charge of handing out construction contracts to private companies. He took bribes and got caught. I was eighteen. My father visited him when he was in the military penitentiary in New Hampshire."

"What happed to Katarina?"

"She divorced him after he got out. I remember when he was living in a one-room basement apartment with a bare bulb hanging from the ceiling on LaSalle Street. It really made me sad."

"Did you ever talk to him about any of this?"

"I only asked him one question: 'What happened to the grand piano?'"

Both women laughed, and Polly said, "Katarina took it."

"Of course. Buck said she sold it for much less than it was worth."

After Polly left, Kitty recalled the time she was six years old, walking on a sidewalk with Buck, who had just graduated from the University of Alabama and was back in Chicago for a brief visit, when a loose, snarling, barking dog approached them. Buck moved in front of Kitty, as he did so shielding her behind him. He spoke calmly to the dog and it slowly backed off, though continuing to growl and bare its big yellow teeth. Buck and Kitty passed by without altering their pace and the dog kept its distance. Kitty asked Buck what he'd said to prevent it from attacking them and he told her, "It wasn't what I said, it was how I said it."

The light had gone but Kitty did not turn on a lamp. If the phone rang she wouldn't answer it.

Katarina

Beautiful Enough

Kitty's doctor's prescription for her nervous condition was to "go somewhere warm and lie in the sun. It'll help you relax and heal the sores on your skin. Rub in the ointment I gave you three or four times a day and the eczema will clear up in a couple of weeks. You need to get away from this cold weather."

Kitty told her husband, Rudy, what the doctor said, and she and their five-year-old son, Roy, left Chicago two days later. They moved into a suite at the Casa Tropical Hotel on Cayo Divino three hundred miles south of Miami. Most of the citizens of Cayo Divino in 1950 were Cuban or of Cuban descent. Visitors to the island were usually either sport fishermen or people who needed to disappear for a while. Rudy had friends who got lost down there until it was okay for them to go back to wherever they came from. Other than a few bars and a small aquarium there wasn't much to offer in the way of amusement; for that there was a ferry once a day to Havana that took eleven hours.

Cayo Divino had not completely recovered from the Great Depression of the 1930s; many locals made a living salvaging wreckage off sunken or disabled ships. Other than that the only regular work was in the four resort hotels. Kitty wanted peace and quiet. Rudy, who often had business to conduct in Havana, told her to stay in Florida for as long as it took for her to get better; he promised to stop in Cayo Divino for a few days to or from there to Chicago. She sunbathed, swam in the Atlantic Ocean and slept well. Roy played with the Cuban kids who lived around the hotel, got to know the employees and enjoyed meeting and talking to the other guests.

Late one morning Kitty was sitting in a lounge chair on the lawn behind the hotel reading a magazine when a man approached her.

"Pardon me, Miss. I don't mean to disturb you, but I believe I've seen you before."

Kitty looked up at him.

"Have we met?"

"No. You're in the movies, aren't you?"

"You're mistaken. I only go to the movies."

"My name is Guy Rubenstein, from New York. You certainly could be."

"Could be what?"

"In the movies. You're beautiful enough."

"I'm Kitty, from Chicago. And I'm Mrs., not Miss."

"Twice mistaken. I'm sorry to have bothered you, Kitty from Chicago."

Kitty and Roy at the Casa Tropical Hotel

He walked away. Good looking, Kitty thought, in a slightly slithery Zachary Scott kind of way. Tall but not too tall, slender but probably strong. Jewish. Unusual first name for a Jew. The only man she knew of named Guy was Guy Madison, the cowboy actor.

That afternoon she and Roy were having lunch in the hotel dining room when Guy Rubenstein came in. As he passed their table he said hello to Kitty.

"Do you know that man?" asked Roy.

"No. He spoke to me earlier, when I was outside reading."

"I saw him yesterday in front of the hotel kissing a woman. She got into a limousine going to Miami. After it drove away another woman came out of the hotel and he kissed her, too."

"Did she also leave in a limo?"

"I don't know. I went to meet up with Chico and Jorge. Who is he?"

Guy Rubenstein

"Nobody, honey. Just another guy."

The next time Kitty saw Rubenstein was the following evening. He was sitting on a stool at the hotel bar with one arm around a blonde. Roy was with his mother and she asked him if that woman was one of the two he'd seen Guy Rubenstein kissing two days before.

"No. One of them had black hair and the other one's hair was sort of dark red, like yours. Why?"

"Oh, I was just wondering how I'd look as a blonde."

Lefty's Hat

"Dad, do you know who that guy is? He's been standing on the corner across the street all morning."

Roy's father came out of the door to his liquor store and looked at the man.

"No, son, I don't think so. He's either waiting for someone who's late to meet him or maybe he's got nowhere to go."

"Everyone's got someplace to go, don't they?"

Rudy looked at Roy, who was five years old.

"No, not everyone. They just drift."

"I like being alone sometimes, especially when I'm playing with my toy soldiers on the floor in my room."

Rudy looked again at the man on the corner. He was in his forties or fifties, wearing a shabby dark blue overcoat with the collar turned up.

"It's windy, Dad, he doesn't have a hat. Can we buy him one?"

"Today is Sunday, the stores are closed. Wait here."

Roy stood alone in the doorway for a few minutes. When his father came back he was holding a battered gray double-indented fedora. He handed it to Roy.

"Here, this hat belonged to Lefty Lefkowitz. He left it downstairs. Take it over and give it to that guy."

"What if Lefty comes back for it?"

"He won't be back."

"How do you know?"

"Don't get run over."

Roy crossed the street and held out the hat to the man, who

looked at him for a moment before accepting it. The man put it on his head, said something to Roy, then walked away. Roy came back without being run over.

"What did he say to you?"

" 'Cut off my legs and call me Shorty. It fits!' "

Rudy smiled. "You did a good thing, son. How do you feel now?"

Roy walked into the store without answering him and sat down on a stack of day-old newspapers. Rudy did not ask him again.

Lefty's Hat

An Argument for the Existence of God

Kitty's cousin Lurleen had always been jealous of her. Lurleen envied Kitty's superior good looks, her early success as a model, her talent as a pianist, and her ability to attract handsome and wealthy suitors without trying. Lurleen's marriage to a man who worked without complaint for her father in his jewelry business did nothing to assuage her envy of Kitty, even though both of her cousin's marriages ended in divorce before she was thirty. She also disliked Kitty's six-year-old son, Roy, for no reason other than that he paid no attention to her.

The women lived in the same apartment building on Chicago's west side, which afforded Lurleen ample opportunity to observe the comings and goings of Kitty's visitors. Lurleen was two years older and felt entitled to criticize and reprimand Kitty for what Lurleen considered her younger cousin's improper behavior, most often involving men.

During a party in Kitty's apartment, Lurleen's husband, Herbert, got into an argument with Morgan Barnes, one of Kitty's boyfriends. Herbert, a short, pudgy man, accused Morgan, who was six inches taller and in decidedly better physical condition than himself, of having insulted Lurleen by suggesting that she take it easy on her drinking. At the moment, she was holding glasses in both of her hands.

"Finish one cocktail before taking another," Morgan told her, "and quit talking trash."

"Mind your own business," Herbert said. "Who do you think you are to order my wife what to do or say?"

Lurleen

"Her remarks about Kitty's choice of men are out of line. She's talking too loud and, in case you haven't noticed, is about to fall down."

Herbert attempted to slap Morgan's face but the larger man grasped Herbert's wrist before he could make contact.

"Unhand my husband, you brute!" shouted Lurleen.

Kitty came over and told her to quiet down.

"You're ruining my party," she said.

Morgan Barnes released Lurleen's husband's hand and spoke to her.

"Both of you had better get out of here before he gets hurt and you're flat on your face."

Kitty could see that her cousin was about to throw one of her drinks at Morgan but before she did Lurleen stopped herself, quickly knocked back what remained of the cocktail in her left hand, and dropped the glass.

"Finish the other one, too," said Kitty, "and go back upstairs."

Lurleen stared at her for a few seconds before staggering toward the door and disappeared, still holding the glass in her right hand. Herbert followed her out of the apartment.

"What's her problem?" Morgan asked Kitty.

"The trouble with women is the feeling of control. They resent it when men automatically take control of a situation, or try to, and they despise what they perceive as weakness when men don't."

Morgan laughed.

"So what's the solution?"

"God didn't intend there to be one. Men and women are not meant to be friends."

"I thought we were friends," said Morgan.

Kitty looked at him.

"I've always hated parties," she said.

Detective Story

Roy had never before met a private detective. Jimmy Boyle told him that Wendy Delmonico's father had been a cop for a few years, then quit and opened up his own detective agency. The Delmonicos had recently moved into the neighborhood, a bungalow on Maplewood Street, two blocks away from Roy's house. Wendy was eleven years old, the same age as Jimmy and Roy, but she attended a private school in a suburb of Chicago so they did not see her very often.

"How do you know?" Roy asked Jimmy.

"My old man told my mother a couple of days ago. 'You know that family just bought Pat Sheehan's old house?' she said. 'What about 'em?' my old man asked. 'The father's a private dick, a detective. His name is Al Delmonico. Bob Johnson knew him when they was both on the force. They protected President Eisenhower when he came here.'"

"Wendy Delmonico's sister invited my sister to her birthday party. She'll be six on Saturday. My mother wants me to walk Margie over there and pick her up when the party's over."

"How'd Margie meet her?"

"At the park."

"Maybe you'll get to meet her old man. I bet he carries a rod. Ask him to show it to you."

"He probably won't even be there."

On Saturday Roy accompanied his sister to the Delmonico house; they climbed the front steps and Roy rang the doorbell. Mrs. Delmonico opened the door. She had a high pile of jet-black hair on her head, big dangling silver earrings, and bloodred lipstick spread on and around her mouth.

"Hi, Margie," she said, "the girls are in the dining room."

Margie ran past her into the house.

"And you must be her brother."

"Yes, ma'am. I'm Roy."

"Hello, Roy. It's noon now. The party will be over by four. Will you be coming back for Margie?"

Roy nodded.

"Well, thank you, Roy. See you then."

She closed the door and Roy went back down the stairs. As he did, a dark green Chrysler sedan pulled up in front of the house and a tall man wearing a blue suit and tie and a wide-brimmed gray hat got out.

"Hello, son," he said as he approached the front steps.

Four hours later Roy returned to the house and again rang the doorbell. This time the tall man, now hatless and coatless, in his shirtsleeves with his tie loosened, opened the door.

"I'm here to pick up my sister Margie," Roy said.

"Come in. The girls are still opening presents."

The man, whom Roy assumed was the birthday girl's father, followed Roy into the house. Roy stood next to him in the living room listening to the girls squeal and chatter. Mrs. Delmonico appeared and quickly came over to Roy.

"As you can hear," she said, "the festivities are still in progress, but I believe Trudy has just opened her last gift. Would you like a piece of cake? It's angel food, Trudy's favorite."

"No, thank you, Mrs. Delmonico. I'll just wait here."

Roy noticed that attached to the tall man's belt was a small brown leather holster from which the black handle of a gun protruded. The holster was snapped shut and rode high on the man's right hip. Mr. Delmonico went into the dining room and began gathering up discarded wrapping paper and cardboard boxes. He crumpled up the torn paper and ribbons then walked back past Roy and out the front door. He came back in and stood next to Roy. The detective's holster was on a level with Roy's head. He looked at it and noticed that it was unsnapped. Roy figured the snap must have been dislodged by accident, perhaps when Trudy's father had bent down while crumpling and folding the wrapping papers.

"Mr. Delmonico?"

"Yes, son?"

"Your holster is open."

The detective looked down, saw that it was and snapped it closed just as Margie came over to Roy and said, "The party's over now. I can go."

"Did you thank Mrs. Delmonico?"

Margie nodded and walked out the front door. When they were on the sidewalk Roy asked her if she had had a good time.

"It was okay. I didn't really know any of the other girls. A colored man came in while we were singing 'Happy Birthday' and said something to Trudy's father. Mr. Delmonico took his gun out of its holster, so did the other man, and followed him outside. They were gone for a while, then Mr. Delmonico came back in."

"Did you hear any shots being fired?"

Margie shook her head.

The next day Roy told Jimmy Boyle what Margie had told him.

"My old man says a cop pulls his weapon only when he's going to use it. Do you think the colored guy is Mr. Delmonico's partner?"

"How would I know?"

"I didn't think colored guys were allowed to be private eyes."

"Why wouldn't they be? They can be cops and soldiers."

A week later Roy saw Wendy Delmonico walking on Maplewood toward her house. He said hello to her.

"Hi, Roy. Did your sister have fun at Trudy's party?"

"I guess so. I thought maybe you would be there."

"I was at my school, taking a French lesson for extra credit."

"Is your father really a private detective?"

"Yes. He used to be a policeman."

"Does he have a partner? A colored man?"

"Johnny Bright. He used to be a policeman, too. How did you know he works with my father?"

"He came into your house for a couple of minutes while my sister was there, then he and your dad went out together."

"Johnny's really nice, and he's very smart. My father told me that he was the first Negro to graduate from Northwestern University. One of the first, anyway."

That night at dinner Roy told his mother what Wendy had said about Johnny Bright.

"He must be an extraordinary man," said Kitty. "It's unusual for a black man and a white man to be in business together. You say they're private detectives?"

"Uh huh. They carry guns."

"I went to Mexico City once with your father. I didn't like it. Everybody there carries a gun. People get murdered all the time. Your father said the killers hardly ever go to jail because they pay off the cops and the judges."

"Jimmy's father told him a policeman takes out his gun only if he's going to use it."

"I've only met Mrs. Delmonico once. She had her hair piled high on her head."

"She still does."

Roy did not tell his mother about Mr. Delmonico and Johnny Bright running out of the house during the birthday party with guns in their hands.

One afternoon four months later Al Delmonico's and Johnny Bright's bodies were found riddled with bullets seated in Delmonico's Chrysler parked on an abandoned pier on the

Calumet River. Mrs. Delmonico and her daughters moved out of the house on Maplewood Street that night.

"Nobody I've talked to knows where they are now," Kitty told Roy. "We might as well be living in Mexico City."

Al Delmonico

The Old Graveyard

Roy passed by or cut through the old graveyard every day on his way to and from grammar school. There were two graves side by side that he stopped at frequently, pausing to read the names of the interred and the epitaphs inscribed on their tombstones. Tendresse and Pierre Raffolet were buried in Chicago in 1913. Tendresse had been born in 1895, Pierre in 1894, both in Paris, France. Their epitaphs were: for Pierre, "La mort passe, mais il reste"; and for Tendresse, "La mort passe, mais elle reste." The second time he noticed these graves, Roy copied the epitaphs into his school notebook.

His mother had taken French in high school and kept a French-English dictionary on a bookshelf in the living room of their apartment. Roy looked up the words and translated them as "Death passes by, but he remains" and "Death passes by, but she remains." When his mother came home from work that afternoon Roy showed her the epitaphs and his renderings and asked her if the translations were correct.

"I'm pretty rusty with my French now, Roy," she said, "but I think you've got it right."

"I looked up the meanings of their names, too. Raffolet means 'to be passionately fond.'"

"Crazy about," said his mother.

"And Tendresse means 'tenderness.'"

"Or 'caresses.'"

"Pierre means 'stone.'"

"Roy, you've really done a great job!"

Girl in French movie

"They were both from France and died very young, Pierre at nineteen and Tendresse at eighteen. I'd like to know why they came to Chicago and how come they died so young."

"They may have been in an accident, in a car or on a train. I don't know, Roy, unless of course they wanted to get married and their parents wouldn't let them. It's possible that they committed suicide together. What puzzles me is their names. Were those their real names or were they given to each other. It's a mystery. They must have been madly in love."

"Maybe their ghosts rise from their graves after dark so they can be together again, curling around each other like Casper the Friendly Ghost does with other ghosts sometimes."

The idea of the couple's double suicide bothered Roy, he really couldn't understand it. If their families forbade them from marrying, they could have run away to another city, or even back to France. Roy also wondered what France was like, what people did there that was different from life in America. They spoke French, of course, used words Roy could not pronounce properly. Why didn't everyone in the world speak the same language? Once his mother was watching a French movie on TV and Roy watched a few minutes of it. A beautiful girl wearing only a white slip was sitting on a chair in front of a mirror brushing her hair while she was smoking a cigarette and talking on the phone. Nothing else happened while Roy watched, the camera never moved and the girl did not remove the cigarette from her mouth. Her lips were like two fat snails crawling so slowly atop one another that even though she was speaking it seemed that they did not move, either. Her hair was light-colored, probably blonde, and fell almost to her shoulders. Did Tendresse have blonde hair?

The old graveyard, Roy decided, was a foreign country, too.

Yukon Story

Roy's Uncle Buck, his mother's brother, who was fourteen years older than Kitty, had been working in Alaska building a railroad through the Yukon Territory when he got pleurisy and came to stay with his sister, mother, and Roy at their apartment in Chicago while he recuperated. Buck was forty years old then, a civil and mechanical engineer. He'd been in the Yukon for three months through the late fall and early winter of 1952. Roy was seven and enjoyed listening to his uncle's stories about clearing forests and laying down tracks, hearing moose calls and wolf howls during the long frigid nights, and the occasional fights among the laborers that sometimes involved gun battles.

"Were any of the men killed?" Roy asked him.

"Only one that I know of, nephew. Almost everybody up there carries a gun or a knife."

"Did you?"

"Yes, a .357. It's in my duffel bag."

"I don't want a gun in my house," said Rose, Roy's grandmother.

"Don't worry, Ma," Buck said, "it's locked in a case and unloaded."

They were all in the kitchen. Roy's mother was frying eggs and bacon on the stove for breakfast.

"Put on a shirt, son," Rose told Buck, "it's freezing cold in here."

Buck was wearing only pajama bottoms and his feet were bare.

He laughed and said, "Cold? This isn't cold. It was thirty below in the Yukon."

Buck picked up a strip of bacon from a wrapper on the counter, held it in front of his face, and took a bite.

"Buck!" Kitty shouted. "You can't eat raw bacon! You'll get sick."

"All the boys up north eat it right out of the package."

Buck nibbled the bacon until he'd devoured the entire strip.

"Your uncle's crazy, Roy," said Kitty. "Don't do what he does."

"Did you see any wolves, Unk?"

"A few, but they mostly kept their distance from our camp. Noise from the trucks, skinners, and bulldozers frightened them away."

"Are you going back after you feel better?"

"I don't think so, Roy. It's already the middle of January and the job is scheduled to wrap up in March."

Buck was divorced; his eleven–year-old son, Kip, had been sent by his mother, Katarina, to live with her father, Doc Wurtzel, in Mexico until she was resettled. Katarina was an alcoholic, so Buck thought it was better for Kip to live for now at Doc's hacienda in Cuernavaca.

"Are you going to live in Chicago?"

"I'm going to open an office downtown, nephew, and start my own engineering firm. I want to work for myself from now on."

"Come on," said Kitty, "let's all sit down and eat. The coffee's ready, Buck."

"One of our sled dogs bit a thermos in half one morning and scalded himself so bad that he was blinded and had to be shot. Big husky named Bulletproof. The ground was frozen so hard he couldn't be buried, so the Eskimo boys skinned and ate him."

"Did you eat dog, Unk? How did it taste?"

"Buck will tell you later, Roy," said his grandmother. "Finish your eggs."

Years later, after his mother, grandmother, and Buck were dead, Roy found the steel-toed boots his uncle had worn when he was in the Yukon in a steamer trunk in the garage of Kitty's house. The leather was stiff, of course, but Roy tried them on anyway. They were too small for Roy, which surprised him because he always thought of Buck as being bigger than he was. Nothing else in the trunk could Roy identify as having belonged to his uncle. The boots had probably been packed away in there since the winter of '52.

Roy remembered his uncle telling him that one of the work crew in the Yukon, a man named Morrison, told Buck that when he was nineteen years old, laying track in Nome, he'd gotten frost-bite so extreme that he'd had to have all of the toes on his left foot amputated. Morrison learned how to walk by putting most of his weight on his right foot, balancing on the toes. The bones in the small toes of that foot kept breaking, though, so when he was twenty-six, he cut them off himself with a hacksaw. He left the big toe attached. Buck asked Morrison how long ago he'd lopped off four of the toes on his right foot and Morrison said, "Must be eight since I'm thirty-four now." He went on to tell Buck that get-ting rid of those toes had improved his balance. He always stuffed a heavy sock inside the front of his boots. Buck asked Morrison why he hadn't cut off the big toe, too. "Just in case," said Morrison. "In case of what?" asked Buck. Morrison laughed and said, "You never know when another toe could come in handy."

MORRISON

Arthur The Wolf Wolf

"You hear about The Wolf?"

"What about him?"

"He got arrested yesterday. Two plainclothes cops dragged him out of Miss Collier's classroom in front of everybody."

"For what?"

"Stealin' Peppy Prezant's watch out of his locker. My next-door neighbor, Beverly Silva, told me Martha Pettegolo saw him do it while Peppy was at baseball practice. Apparently The Wolf's been liftin' stuff from lockers for a long time."

Arthur "The Wolf" Wolf looked like his name. He had a lopsided grin and his tongue hung out of his mouth even while he was talking.

"He'll probably get thrown into reform school in St. Charles," Richie Gates told Roy. "That's what Beverly said happened to Mickey Stutz when he got nailed coppin' hubcaps in the teachers' parking lot."

Richie and Roy were in the seventh grade at Torquemada Grammar School. Beverly Silva was in the eighth, as was The Wolf.

"I almost got into a fight with him at the softball field, remember?" Roy said. "He got caught goin' through the pockets of jackets kids playin' in the game left on the benches. I threatened to kneecap him with a bat."

"Yeah, I do. I guess we won't be seein' him around for a while."

The Wolf spent six months in St. Charles. Two weeks after he got out he bought a Harrington & Richardson .25 caliber pistol from a Puerto Rican guy on Maxwell Street and shot his stepfather three times in the back, then shot himself in the head. His mother wasn't home at the time. The cops told her it was probably a good thing; there was one bullet left in the gun that might have been intended for her. She said she didn't think so and gave them a note her son had left for her.

> *Dear Mother your husband aint going*
> *to beat me or you up again he was a*
> *bad guy so am I nobody will miss us*
> *I have another weapon in this chamber*
> *it is a sword of Spain*
> *love Arthur*

"Why do you think The Wolf knocked himself off?" Richie asked Roy. "He could have just stolen some money out of his mother's purse and run away. Did you see the note he left for her? It was in the newspaper."

"My grandfather read it to me," said Roy. "He told me the part about Spain is from *Othello*, Shakespeare's play."

"Yeah, Beverly says we'll have to read it next year when we're in eighth grade."

Arthur "The Wolf" Wolf

Visitors

Roy's little sister, Sally, began seeing apparitions when she was four or five years old. Roy was fifteen when she first told him about a woman who appeared in her room standing at the foot of her bed. Roy asked her what she looked like.

"She's about the same age as Mom, but she doesn't look like her. She has blonde hair, almost white, and she's wearing a white dress."

"You've seen her more than once?"

"Yes, she's standing in the hallway now outside my room. Sometimes she comes in."

"Does she speak to you?"

"Not always. She's nice, she wants to know if I feel all right."

"What's her name?"

"I don't know, she's never told me. I call her Rose, our grand-mother's name, because she died before I was born. I can pretend that's who she is."

"Nanny didn't have blonde hair, it was brown. She wasn't so nice to me. Your visitor must not be Nanny's ghost."

Sally was lying in bed when she told Roy about the phantom woman.

"I haven't told anyone else about her, only you. Should I tell Mom?"

"That's up to you, Sal. You know she believes there are spirits around her sometimes."

"What are spirits?"

"Mom thinks they're the souls of dead people. They can appear as ghosts that only Mom can see."

"Do they talk to her?"

"Ask Mom."

"Have you ever seen them?"

"No, Sal, I haven't. Do you want to get up now and have breakfast with me?"

Sally shook her head.

"I want to stay in bed. Rose might come back."

"Okay, I'll be in the kitchen. Mom's still sleeping. Call if you want me."

Roy left the room. His mother, Kitty, came into the kitchen while he was eating a bowl of cereal.

"Good morning, Roy. I heard you talking to someone. Was anyone here?"

"I asked Sally if she was hungry."

"No, it wasn't her voice."

Kitty sat down at the table. She had gauze bandages wrapped around her hands and arms up to her elbows. She wore bandages during the night to cover the gooey ointment she rubbed over her eczema sores so it wouldn't get on her sheets and pillows.

"Sally sees ghosts, did you know that? She talks to them. To one, at least."

Kitty's brown eyes were cloudy, almost grey. She had not yet brushed her hair or pencilled in her eyebrows.

"When did she tell you this?"

"Just now, when I was in her room."

"The one she talks to, is it Nanny?"

"No, it's a woman about your age who has blonde hair. Sally calls her Rose, though."

Kitty began unwrapping the bandages. She winced as she pulled them away from her skin.

"Oh, I'm sorry, Roy, you're eating. I'll undo these in my bedroom. My sores are itching."

"It's okay, Ma, I'm almost finished."

"Mary Ann, her name is Mary Ann. The blonde woman who visits Sally."

"How do you know?"

"Ouch, the bandages always stick to my arms."

Mary Ann

Who Shot John

"Like I told the officer, this girl was on the street. Young, pretty, blonde, but dirty. I mean filthy, like she hadn't washed her face and most probably the rest of her in weeks. She was pushin' a shopping cart, had clothes in it, shoes, other stuff."

"What other stuff?"

"Hairbrush, comb, broken umbrella. She asked me could I help her. It was rainin', not real hard, a gloomy afternoon, nobody else around."

"Help her how?"

"She said she needed a place to stay, that she got thrown out of where a guy she knew lived."

"Did she tell you why he'd made her leave?"

"Somethin' about an argument. She offered to have sex with me if I took her in."

"How old are you, Mr. Kozinsky?"

"Forty-two."

"The girl is seventeen. What did you do then?"

"Like I said, she was real pretty, had on a little skirt, her blouse was mostly unbutttoned, and she was barefoot. I thought it might be okay if she had a bath, I admit it, but there were too many things wrong. I didn't know she was that young."

"What things?"

"She could be a junkie, a thief, or just plain nuts, I don't know. I gave her ten dollars."

"Is that when the kid showed up?"

"Yeah, right then. He come runnin' around the corner. Eleven, twelve years old, my guess."

"He's twelve."

"Shoutin' there's a guy lookin' for a girl stole somethin' from him, wavin' a gun."

"We've talked to the kid. His name's Roy, lives in the neighborhood."

"What about the guy chasin' after her?"

"We got him, holding him on a weapons charge."

"That's when I split, soon as I heard the word gun. The kid tell you?"

"He did."

"What about the girl? She all right?"

"She's in custody. Her head's messed up. You can go now."

Kozinsky stood up.

"Sergeant?"

"What?"

"Can I get my ten dollars back?"

Mr. Kozinsky

Saturday in the House of God

Harmon Mangel's family moved into Roy's neighborhood a week after the Pedersen house burned down. The Mangels rented a third-floor apartment on Menominee Street a few doors down from the scorched remains. Harmon was ten years old, the same age as Roy. He was a short, scrawny kid who wore glasses and had crewcut red hair. When Roy asked him what his favorite sport was Harmon replied, "I like baseball, but I'm not a very good player."

"I'll help you get better," Roy said. "Baseball's my favorite sport, too. I'm the shortstop on our team. I want to be like Luís Aparicio, the rookie shortstop on the White Sox."

"What's the name of your team?"

"The Scorpions. We play mostly at Heart-of-Jesus park. Have you been there?"

Harmon shook his head.

"I'll take you. You can meet all the guys."

Roy did not see Harmon Mangel often, so he never did take him to the park. Whenever Roy offered to play baseball with him, Harmon said he had to study or go to Hebrew school or to the synagogue with his parents.

"What's a synagogue?" asked Roy.

"A temple. It's where our family goes to worship. We're Orthodox Jews."

"My mother's a Catholic, she goes to St. Tim's. Where's your temple?"

"On Warsaw Avenue, next door to a candy store."

Harmon Mangel

"Oh yeah, Kapp's. They have good doughnuts and pinball machines. Have you gone in there?"

"No. My parents don't want me to eat candy."

"I've never been in a synagogue. Can I go with you sometime?"

"Probably. I'll ask my father."

A couple of weeks later, on a Friday after school, Harmon told Roy he could go with him to the synagogue the next morning if he wanted to.

"Saturday is an important day in our religion. The temple will be full."

"I asked my mother what an Orthodox Jew is and she said she wasn't sure. She said she passed by your temple once and saw a lot of people dressed in black standing around in front of it."

"Meet me at my house tomorrow morning at nine o'clock," said Harmon. "We'll walk over together."

Harmon
Mangel's
father

The synagogue was a one-story yellow building squeezed in between two six-flat apartment houses.

"You'll have to wear a yarmulke to go in," Harmon told Roy. "I brought an extra one for you."

Harmon took two black beanie-sized caps out of a pocket of his coat and handed one to Roy.

"Here, put it on toward the back of your head. You have to keep it on while you're inside."

"Why?"

"To be humble in the house of God. It's how you show respect for Him."

"God doesn't live here," said Roy.

"He lives in the hearts and minds of His chosen people."

"Is He a Jew?"

"He must be."

"What about Jesus?"

"Jesus was Jewish and He was God's son."

Roy followed Harmon into the synagogue. Every seat was filled and dozens of bearded men were standing in the aisles holding an open book and mumbling in a language Roy did not understand. A low hanging balcony was suspended over the room. It was so low Roy was afraid that it might collapse.

"Who sits up there?" he asked Harmon.

"Women. Only men are allowed to sit downstairs. The men and women never sit together."

Roy looked up at the balcony. Every woman was holding a book open and mumbling like the men. All of them were wearing black dresses and had black scarves or shawls over their heads. The men below were wearing big black hats. Most of the boys had long wispy sideburns that curled out from their heads. The light in the room was dim and it was very hot, so hot that Roy began to sweat. Despite the heat almost all of the men wore heavy black overcoats. Roy could barely see the front where there was a low stage upon which several men were standing, reading, mumbling and repeatedly nodding their heads.

Roy felt trapped. If there were a fire he knew that he would be trampled to death. He looked around for Harmon but didn't see him. Roy figured that he had gone to sit or stand by his father and that his mother must be in the balcony. Roy was suffocating, he had to get out. He squeezed himself like a snake through the sea of overcoats back to the door through which he and Harmon had entered and pushed it open. Once he was on the sidewalk and able to breathe normally again Roy took off the beanie, stuffed it into a back pocket of his trousers and began to run.

He did not stop running until he'd gone the six blocks to Heart-of-Jesus park. Kids were already playing ball on one of the two diamonds, so Roy sat down on a bench to watch them.

His friend Winky Wicklow, a fellow Scorpion, came over and sat down next to him.

"Hey, Roy. I thought maybe you weren't gonna play today. We've got a game against the Gophers on the other field at ten-thirty. You left your glove at my house yesterday. I brought it with me."

"I'll play," said Roy.

"What's wrong? You don't look so good. You feelin' okay?"

"I just escaped from Dracula's castle. I thought I was gonna die."

Winky laughed. "What're you talkin' about?"

"Vampires, man. I was trapped in a room full of vampires. It was the creepiest place I've ever been."

"You're crazy, Roy. Dracula's castle isn't real. And even if it was it wouldn't be around here."

"I was crazy to have gone there. Anyhow, I got away."

Roy stood up and took the beanie out of his back pocket.

"What's that?" Winky asked.

Roy walked over to a garbage can and tossed the cap into it. Winky got up and stood next to him.

"You must've had a bad dream, huh, Roy? I've had some. Once I dreamed that my sister Mary was boiling human ears and fingers in a big pot on the stove in our kitchen."

Roy watched a batter hit a line drive into the gap between left and center.

"He's runnin' like his hair's on fire," Winky said.

"I know the feeling," said Roy. "Let's go play catch."

Big Things

Roy's friend Paulie Dnieper wanted to be a priest. He was thirteen, a year and a half older than Roy. His father, Big Paul, was a handyman, and Paulie lived with him, his mother, Marta, and older sister, Julia, in the basement apartment of a building down the alley from Roy's house. Paulie's father and mother had both been born and raised in Poland; their families emigrated to Chicago when Big Paul and Marta were in their late teens. The two boys were sitting on the ground in the doorway of the Dniepers' apartment drinking orange Nehi sodas. It was warm for April but windy, rain was on its way.

"We got the game in just in time," said Roy.

"Yeah, good thing we started early."

"Why do you want to be a priest?" Roy asked.

"I won't have to empty garbage cans and unplug drains for a living. The church will take care of me when I get old."

"Do you believe in God?"

Paulie took a big slug of his Nehi.

"Sure," he said. "Don't you?"

"My mother says if there's really a God He wouldn't let guys like Hitler murder millions of people."

"God's got a reason for everything He does. He made us, didn't He?"

"Our parents made us."

"How'd they do it? By magic?"

"They put their bodies together and our fathers stirred the pot."

"With what? What pot?"

"I don't know exactly. Didn't your father tell you how?"

"He doesn't talk about big things. He's a janitor."

"What about your mother?"

"You kiddin'?"

"How about Julia? She's sixteen, and her tits are gettin' big."

"I don't look at 'em."

Roy finished off his bottle of pop and got to his feet.

"You gonna keep your bottle?" asked Paulie. "I can get two cents for it."

Roy handed him his empty.

"See ya," he said.

By the time Roy got to the back gate of his house there were puddles in the cracks in the alley. He wished he had a big sister.

The next time Roy was at Paulie's house, Big Paul, wearing dirty overalls and a woollen shirt with the sleeves rolled up to his elbows, said to him, "Why you ask Paulie he want be priest and about God exist?"

Roy looked up at Big Paul. There were holes in his face, black circles with spikelike hairs sticking out of them. His blue eyes were small with tiny red dots in the whites. Big Paul's hair was a scrub brush with brown bristles erect as infantrymen at attention.

Roy shrugged his shoulders. "I never knew a kid before who wanted to be a priest."

"What you talk about Hitler?"

"He killed a lot of people, didn't he?"

"German army invade my country, murder my uncles and cousins."

Big Paul rubbed his thick fingers back and forth through the scrub brush.

"You smart boy, huh?"

"I don't know," said Roy.

"What work your father do?"

"Nothing. He's dead."

Big Paul bent forward and gripped Roy's shoulders with his large hands. Roy thought that if he wanted to Big Paul could push his body straight down through the floor into the earth below.

"You want talk sometime you come me, okay?"

Roy nodded.

Big Paul held onto him for what seemed to Roy a very long time.

BIG PAUL

Baseball

"Last night I watched a weird movie about Dracula's daughter. She bit into women's necks and drank their blood like her father, only she just attacked girls and women, never boys or men."

"Do you think that means she likes to have sex with other women?"

"I don't know. There are guys who go for other guys, so it probably goes for women, too."

Roy and Jimmy Boyle were sitting on the outfield grass at Heart-of-Jesus park after their game against the Artesian Street Rockets. Roy was ten years old, Jimmy was eleven.

"Dracula's daughter looked a lot like Miss Freddezza. Remember her?"

"Yeah, I had her in third grade. She wore long, black dresses and a black wig that tilted to one side or the other. She was mean to all the boys in our class. I guess she could be one of those kind of women."

"Dracula's daughter had bushy dark eyebrows and dark eyes and most of the time held the edge of a cape over her mouth and nose, uncovering her face only when she bent down to bite a girl."

"Do you know how women have sex with each other?"

Roy didn't answer Jimmy right away. He looked across the park to where two women were walking together pushing baby buggies ahead of them.

"I'm not sure," Roy said.

"Homos play with other guys' weenies," said Jimmy. "That's what my cousin Neal told me, but girls don't got weenies."

Roy liked girls, he knew that, but he didn't know much about sex, what people, male or female, actually did. He watched the women pushing their buggies slowly along the sidewalk that encircled the field. One of them had long blonde hair, the other was a brunette with her hair pulled back in a bun. They were talking and laughing. It was better to think about baseball.

A few days later, while Roy was making himself a peanut butter and jelly sandwich in the kitchen of his house, he overheard his mother talking on the telephone in the hallway.

"Yes, Diana, but I don't trust him. There's always been something about Lou Drexel that isn't right.

"Okay, I understand, he's handsome and all that, but he lied about Monique. 'Kitty,' he said, 'I've never even met her.'

"It wasn't a mistake, honey. He got her pregnant, then paid for the abortion. You don't forget that if it happened two or even ten years ago.

Diana

Lou
Drexel

"You keep saying that. So he's a hunk and can keep a girl happy, for a while, anyway. And Monique didn't kill herself.

"No, I'm not saying that Lou killed her. I don't know exactly what happened, neither did the cops. He's poison, Diana."

"I get it. He gives you orgasms, good for you.

"Diana, are you there?"

Roy's mother hung up the phone. She came into the kitchen chewing her lower lip.

"What happened, Ma? Is Diana all right?"

"She hung up on me."

Kitty turned around and walked out of the kitchen. Roy bit into his sandwich. It needed more jelly.

Catholic Girls

When Kitty was told that Our Lady of Everlasting Obedience was closing and the building and property sold she was shocked and upset.

"Not enough people go to church anymore," said June DeLisa. "The parishioners are being told to go to St. Mona's."

" 'The Moaners' we used to call them. That's ten miles away, it's a hardship for our old neighborhood. People could just walk over. What excuse do they have for closing?"

"Money, what else?"

"The Pope's not broke."

"Business, Kitty. The church is a business, like everything else. If customers stop coming, the shop gets shut."

"People don't believe in God the way they used to."

June laughed and lit a cigarette. "Why should they?"

Kitty stood up and looked out the living room window.

"When we were girls we thought the nuns knew everything. They didn't know anything. Neither did we. Dumb Chicago Catholic girls, kept in the dark."

"Oh, Kitty, don't be so drastic. They thought they were living pure lives."

"Tell that to the babies they buried."

"It's the priests who should have been buried."

Both women sipped their Bloody Marys.

"It's beginning to rain. I'll drive over to the school and pick up Roy. He didn't take a hat this morning."

"It's no good to always think that things were better in the old days. We just didn't know better."

"Do we now?"

Kitty carried her half empty glass into the kitchen, then came out and reached into the hall closet.

"I'll be back in ten minutes. Make yourself another drink."

June finished off the one she had, got up and put on her red corduroy jacket.

"I should have worn a raincoat. Remember, Kitty, tomorrow at seven at Pat and Harry's."

"If Rudy doesn't get back tonight from Havana, I may not make it."

"You can get someone to stay with Roy, can't you? Aren't there girls who babysit anymore?"

"I'll try."

Driving to Roy's school Kitty tried to remember the last time she'd gone to church, let alone confession. Damn this rain, she thought. The sun was out in Havana.

June DeLisa

Back Street

"Kitty, are you sure?"

"Of what?"

"That it's safe. That she's qualified."

"Dr. Mantel gave me her number, Polly. I trust him."

"I'd feel better if he were going to do it."

"You know he can't."

"What's her name again?"

"Flores. Señora Liliana Flores."

"She's a foreigner."

"Mexico. Both of our mothers were foreigners."

"Europe is different."

"It's farther from here than Mexico. Try to relax, we'll be at her place soon."

"Did you ever need to do this?"

"No. Even though I knew my marriage wasn't working, I wanted a child."

"Roy is a sweet kid. Did you ever see that movie, *Back Street Girl*, where the girl who's in trouble changes her mind at the last minute, jumps out of her boyfriend's car and runs away? Then at the end you see her holding a small child by the hand walking in a park. Taffy Moore played the girl, a short blonde with big boobs, was always trashy, being knocked around by guys."

Kitty was as nervous as Polly so she drove more slowly than she usually did. The rain had stopped but the sky was black, there were no stars in it. Dr. Mantel said Señora Flores had taken care of a dozen women for him, and who knows how many before she came to Chicago. If there were any sign of danger, Dr. Mantel said, she wouldn't take a risk just for the money.

"You have all small bills, right?"

"Three twenties, four tens, four fives."

Kitty turned off Howard Street onto Paulina and parked across the street from Señora Flores's apartment building. Polly was trembling.

"Take a deep breath, Pol. We can sit here for a few minutes."

Polly shook her head and got out of the car.

"She's on the ground floor, you won't have to walk down any stairs afterwards."

Señora Flores answered the door herself. She was very short, late middle age with a pleasant face. She smiled at the women as she let them in.

"Bienvenidos," she said.

Kitty looked around the front room, which was simply but colorfully furnished, clean and neat. The temperature in the apartment was comfortably warm, not overheated.

"How long will this take?" asked Polly.

"Provided all goes well, not very long. It depends on the bleeding."

Polly took the bills from her purse and handed them to Señora Flores, who accepted them and placed them down on a side table.

"There is fresh coffee on the stove," she told Kitty. "Please to help yourself."

She led Polly to another room and closed the door. Kitty sat down on a lace-covered sofa. Coffee would make her more nervous so she didn't take any. She put a small pillow behind her head, leaned back and fell asleep.

Señora Flores shook her awake gently with a hand on Kitty's left shoulder.

"Is Polly all right?"

"Yes, there is some blood but not to worry. She will be all right. I will give her some things to take. She is resting for a few minutes."

"You told her what to do? How to take care of herself?"

Señora Flores nodded her head. "I believe she understands."

Kitty stood. "I conked out."

Señora Flores handed her a twenty-dollar bill.

When they arrived at Polly's house, Kitty asked her if she needed help walking.

"No, Kitty. I'm a little woozy but better than I thought I might feel. Thank you for everything. It was good of you to drive me home."

"Of course. I wouldn't have let you take a cab alone. Do you have the bag Señora Flores gave you?"

"Right here."

"Call me if you need anything, even if it's the middle of the night."

By the time Kitty got back to her house the rain had started again. She remembered that when she'd gotten pregnant her mother had asked her if she wanted to do something about it.

Polly

Fencing

"You know, Mom, Uncle Buck is a lot like Zorro."

"You mean the Spanish bandit?"

"Zorro isn't a bandit, he robs the evil government officials and distributes the money to poor people."

"Buck isn't a Spaniard."

"No, but he looks like one. He's handsome like Zorro, he has a thin mustache and black hair and knows how to fence. Remember when he taught Johnny McLaughlin and me how to fence in the backyard? His foils and masks are in the black steamer trunk he keeps in our garage."

"My brother is a dashing guy. He loves you and I'm glad he teaches you things your father didn't have time to do."

"Could Dad fence?"

Kitty laughed. "No, of course not. But he could do lots of other things. It's too bad he died before he had a chance to show you. Buck likes doing things with you."

"He wants me to go to Cuba with him."

"You and your dad had good times there. I miss it, too."

"I'd rather live in Havana than here in Chicago. Chico Fernandez and I used to fence with fishing rods."

Kitty thought sometimes that she should get married again. Her brother lived in Florida now, so Roy didn't see him often. A boy needs a father, her mother said. Maybe, but she didn't need a husband. Not yet, anyway. What if Roy and whomever she married didn't get along? She didn't want to think about it.

"How about him?" June DeLisa said to Kitty while they were sipping champagne at Marva Gillespie's cocktail party.

"What about who?"

"Burt Phillips. He and Diane Cortez are on the outs now."

"So?"

"He's always gone for you. And he's loaded."

"When Marva introduced him to me, he asked where I bought my clothes. I thought that was weird."

"What did you say?"

"I asked him where he bought his."

June DeLisa laughed.

"And he doesn't in the least resemble Tyrone Power. I didn't like him."

"Why Tyrone Power?"

"He plays Zorro, Roy's favorite."

"Your brother looks a little like Tyrone Power. Uh oh, here comes Burt Phillips."

"June," he said, "you're looking dangerous, as usual."

"Hello, Burt. You know Kitty, of course."

Before he could say anything, Kitty asked him, "What distinguishes a foil from an épée?"

Phillips stared at Kitty for a few seconds, then walked away.

"Kitty," said June, "you're too cruel."

Kitty took a sip of champagne, then said, "Roy wouldn't like him, either."

Burt Phillips

Pops

"When I was a boy I knew a man in London named Aloysius Gonzaga Jones, named after a Roman saint who died of the plague at the end of the sixteenth century. I ran errands for Aloysius around the East India Docks."

"What kinds of errands?"

"Delivering things to people, small packages, mostly. I didn't know what was in them. Aloysius always carried a pistol in one of his coat pockets. I told him I wanted a pistol, too, in case someone tried to steal a package from me. I was about nine or ten years old then. 'When you're older, Jake,' he told me. He always called me Jake."

"Did he ever let you hold the pistol?"

"Once. It was heavy. Aloysius had big hands, huge hands. The gun looked like a baby's rattle in one of them."

"So you never carried a gun?"

"No, I've never even owned one. There's only one reason to have a gun, Roy, and I hope you never do."

Roy's grandfather, his mother's father, whom Roy called Pops, ate smoked fish for breakfast every morning. He dressed well, wore three piece suits when he sat down at the table. Pops had been born and lived in London, England, until he was in his early twenties. He came to live in Chicago with his daughter, Kitty, and her son, Roy, when he was in his mid-seventies. Pops's name was Jack Colby, he was in the wholesale and retail fur business with his brothers Nate and Ike. Another brother, Louis, was the founder and president of the Chicago Furriers Association. In the 1950s, all of them had offices in the State and Lake Building across the street from the Chicago Theater.

From the age of five Roy considered Pops to be his best friend. He told Roy and Roy's friends stories about his own childhood in London, about growing up poor in the East End on Plumbers Row near the Mile End Road, a market street where Pops and his brothers—there were six of them at that time, two having died before the others emigrated to America—ran errands for the men and women who sold vegetables and fruits from wooden carts. The kids loved Pops's accounts of the Colby brothers' adventures with their pals and adversaries such as Top Hat Tom, Black Harry, Dickie Apples and Pears, and Bob the Knifer.

Roy disliked the stink of smoked fish in the morning, which he refused to eat, but Pops always poured Roy a half cup of coffee with cream and two cubes of sugar in it. Sometimes before breakfast Roy would go into Pops's bathroom with him and pretend to shave with one of his grandfather's razors without a blade in it, soaping his hairless face and making strokes like Pops did. Pops had diabetes, so he tested his urine every morning, passing some into a glass tube along with a solution that turned the mixture gray, a positive result of his condition. Roy did the same, only the liquid in his test tube turned blue, negative evidence of his not having diabetes.

Pops was mugged late one afternoon when he was on his way home, walking the one block from the bus stop to Kitty's house. Two young guys wearing leather jackets and burlap caps assaulted him from

Jack
(Pops)

behind. One grabbed his arms and knocked off his glasses while the other stole Pops's wallet and pocket watch that he kept on a chain attached to his belt, then they ran off. After Pops got to the house, Roy's mother called the police. Two officers showed up, filled out a report and said they'd keep an eye out for the muggers. They were never apprehended and neither Pops's wallet nor pocket watch were recovered.

"I had about thirty dollars in the wallet," Pops told Roy, "and the watch was only of sentimental value. It was a gift to me from Aloysius Jones on my twelfth birthday."

"I'm glad they didn't hurt you," said Roy.

"I'm an old man, I didn't resist."

"If you'd had Aloysius Jones's pistol you could have shot them."

Pops shook his head. "No, Roy, they got the drop on me. But if my friend Bob the Knifer were around, he'd hunt them down and get even for me, and maybe get my watch back."

Roy's grandmother, Rose, from whom Pops had been divorced for many years, died a year before Pops moved into Kitty's house, where she had been living. Because Rose always blamed Pops for their break-up, Kitty was cold to him. She took her father in due to his dire heart condition and close relationship with Roy, whose own father had died soon after Roy's birth.

Shortly before Pops passed away at eighty, he had been relocated by his son, Buck, Kitty's brother, to a nursing facility near his home in Florida. Buck thought the warm climate would be good for his father, and Kitty did not oppose the move. Roy, however, missed his grandfather terribly, and for a time after he learned of Pops's death withdrew from his normal routines. He was not eager to play with his friends and often refused to go to school, claiming that he did not feel well. This wound never did fully heal.

Roy felt the loss of Pops for the rest of his life. Years later, when his mother told Roy that she should not have treated her father so badly, that perhaps she had been unduly and wrongfully influenced by her mother, it meant nothing to Roy. The only thing about Pops that Roy did not miss was the smell of smoked fish in the morning.

POPS

Sons and Sins of the Prophets

Roy wondered why he had dreams and what they meant. Sometimes entire stories took place in his dreams and other times only parts of stories or appearances by people he knew. He was in some of them, usually in places he didn't recognize and in situations he could not completely comprehend. Occasionally dead people appeared, members of his family or their friends. Nothing frightening had happened in his dreams, at least not so far.

The day after he had a confusing dream in which Roy himself, at the age he was now—ten and a half—was lost in an unfamiliar city being followed by a strange man, he asked his grandfather, who lived with him and his mother, what he could do to better understand them.

"They're like movies, Roy. Sometimes they're good, sometimes bad or mysterious, like the one you had last night. There are lots of books by people who insist they can interpret them, mostly based on events that may be occurring in peoples' lives, or occurred in their past."

"Do you have dreams, Pops?"

"Of course, we all do."

"How can I find out who the strange man was who was following me?"

"What did he look like?"

"He was wearing a suit and tie and a hat like my dad sometimes wears."

"A fedora."

"Yeah. He wasn't very tall, about average. I couldn't see his face."

"Did he speak to you?"

"Nobody said anything. I think I heard sounds coming from the streets, cars and streetcars going by."

"Were you afraid of this stranger?"

"I don't know. He didn't come close to me."

"You're certain he was following you? Maybe he was just walking in the same direction as you were."

"I'm sure. In the dream I was sure. But what did it mean?" Roy's grandfather had been reading a book which lay open on his lap.

"Take this book I'm reading about a man named Emanuel Swedenborg, a Swedish theologian, scientist and philosopher. He had a dream that Jesus Christ appeared to him and told him to write a book called *The Heavenly Doctrine*. After that, Swedenborg believed he could visit both heaven and hell and consort with angels and demons. Based on this and other dreams he created a new religion he called Swedenborgianism. He did this two hundred years ago and even today many people believe in his so-called revelations."

"Do you?"

"No, they're just stories. I'm curious about him and other men and women who feel the need to tell people how they should behave and live their lives. It's a type of mania, individuals who get carried away by their delusions. And sometimes it's a collective mania, such as the Sons of the Prophets written about in the Kabbalah, a mystical text of the Jews. There are always people who are looking for answers. Who created the universe? What will happen to them after they die? When men like Swedenborg or Buddha or Muhammad come along and declare that they have the answers, they acquire followers desperate for a belief system."

"Jesus, too?"

"Yes, but I don't think he was so comfortable with it. Believing that he was the son of God, though, once he began proselytizing he couldn't quit."

"Were these prophets all good guys?"

Pops laughed. "Swedenborg seems to have been. I suppose more than a few of these self-proclaimed prophets misbehaved at one time or another. Probably more than a few."

"How did they misbehave?"

"In the usual ways. Coveted and had their way with other men's wives, pocketed money intended by donors for the church. Listen, Roy, why don't you write down your dreams? What of them you can remember, anyway. There may be a pattern that we can discern and enable us to figure out what caused them."

"Do you dream every night?"

"Not every night, no. I did have a dream last night that I remember."

"What was it?"

"A pretty girl with peach-colored hair asked me if I wanted to take a lick of her ice cream cone."

"Did you?"

"That part I don't recall."

"You like chocolate the best, like me. I'll bet if it was chocolate, you did."

Emanuel Swedenborg

Comancheros

"Those black gangs on the South Side got some cool names," said Paddy Riley. "Egyptian Cobras, Devil's Disciples, Heaven's Vampires. We should think up a name like that for our club."

"We got the Scorpions, that's good enough," Winky Wicklow said.

"Scorpions are insects," said Jimmy Boyle, "not scary like cobras or vampires."

"You ever been stung by a scorpion?" asked Roy. "You wouldn't forget it. A kid I knew up in Eagle River almost lost an ear because a scorpion stung him inside it."

"Was it the same kid you said almost died after sticking one of his arms into a bee hive and got stung a hundred times?"

"Earl Weyerholz, yeah."

"He should stay away from anything that crawls or flies."

"He drowned last summer, diving into the river. Hit his head on a rock. Earl was crazy, a daredevil. I liked him."

"Those gangs got lots of members," said Paddy. "They sell drugs and commit robberies. We play ball and have parties."

"You want to hold people up?" asked Winky. "Besides, we only have ten, fifteen guys. The Cobras got over a hundred and most of 'em get shot or go to prison."

"How about Comancheros?" said Roy.

"Who were they?"

"A hundred years ago, maybe more, they were whites and Mexicans who joined up in Texas with the Comanche Indians to steal cattle and raid ranches and do some really bad stuff like kidnap women and sell 'em."

"How do you know about them?"

"I read about the Apache and Comanche Indians. The Comancheros were outlaws. The Mescalero Apaches used to bury their enemies alive up to their necks in hot sand and leave them there to be bitten by insects and burn to death in the desert sun."

"Well, we're not Indians or Mexicans," said Paddy, "and none of us have been in Texas."

"The guys in gangs on the South Side aren't vampires or snakes, either. None of 'em even seen a cobra except in a movie or at the Lincoln Park Zoo."

"Let's think about it more," said Winky.

"The Comancheros and Indians would meet up at Rio de las lenguas, the river of tongues, and in El Valle de las lágrimas, the valley of tears, to divide up what they stole and the kidnapped women."

"Where'd you learn Spanish?" Paddy asked Roy.

Scorpions

"From the Cuban kids I played with in Key West, Florida, when my mother and I lived there."

Roy and his friends did not change their club name, but when the movie *The Comancheros*, starring John Wayne, came to the Nortown Theater, a few of them went with Roy to see it.

Afterwards, Roy said, "They got it all wrong. They made the Comancheros good guys and John Wayne a Texas Ranger rescuing white women, takin' back stolen goods and burning down Indian villages."

Jimmy Boyle said, "I saw John Wayne on TV talking about how white men should take over countries everywhere and civilize the world, that Indians and natives in Africa have to be controlled and put to work."

"John Wayne wouldn't last long walkin' alone on a street on the South Side of Chicago," said Paddy.

Better Than School

"You ever see that old movie on TV where the guy who's a crooked gambler picks up a pretty girl on a train? She gives him kind of a hard time at first but she likes his looks, too, and gets off the train with him. Later she finds out he murdered two people back in the city they just came from. She's already agreed to marry the guy but now decides to run away. She gets a girl who lives in the same apartment building she's been shacked up in with the killer to drive her to another city to catch a train, figuring the guy might look for her at the train station or airport in the city where they've been living. The two girls take off when the guy's not around. When he gets back he notices the other girl's car is gone from its space in the apartment house garage and asks the parking kid about it. The kid tells him the two girls took off together and his girl put a suitcase in the trunk of the car. The girl who's driving told the kid to keep the parking space open, that she'd be back before midnight. He asked her if she had enough gas and she said she had enough to get to Oil City and back."

Roy said to his friend Winky, who was telling him about the movie as they walked to school, "So the killer guesses what's up and drives his car to Oil City."

"Yeah, but before he gets there he sees the other girl in her car alone on the road heading in the other direction. He makes a U-turn and catches up to her and forces her to pull over onto the side of the road. He sticks a gun in her face and she tells him she dropped Lola at the train station in Oil City and that Lola bought a ticket to New York that leaves in two hours. The killer gets back in his car, turns it around again, and drives like a demon."

"He finds her just as she's boarding the train," said Roy, "pulls his piece to shoot her because she's the only one who knows that he committed those murders, but she gets on the train before he can. Then he jumps on the train, finds her, and sits in the seat next to her just as the train begins to move."

"Right!" said Winky. "You seen this movie."

"No, I'm just telling you what I think happens. After the train is rolling, he forces her to go to the ladies room, pushes her in, squeezes himself in with her, and closes the door. He knows if he fires his gun it'll make too much noise and he'll get caught so he starts to strangle her, but he didn't lock the door and a woman passenger opens it."

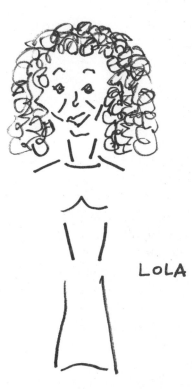

LOLA

"This is better than school! Okay, then what happens?"

"She grabs his gun out of his coat pocket and shoots him."

"No, the woman who opened the door screams and a conductor comes who fights with the killer. Other men come who drag the killer down, and a train cop puts handcuffs on him. They should have ended it the way you said."

"What color hair did Lola have?"

"Dark, it was in black and white. Why?"

"She was a blonde in my movie."

Another Irishman

Roy was on his way to school when he saw a dead man lying on the northwest corner of Desoto and Washtenaw. He was on the southeast corner when he spotted the body so he crossed over to have a closer look. The man was fully dressed, shabby as his coat and trousers were, stretched out flat on his back. His unshaven face was dirt-blackened, his eyes were closed. At first Roy was not certain the man was dead, so he spoke to him.

"Mister, are you dead or sleeping?"

The man did not reply. Roy bent down close to his face and repeated his question. There was still no response. Roy stood up straight and kicked the body lightly with his right foot. The man did not move. Neither was his chest moving, so Roy decided that he wasn't breathing.

The streets were empty except for a woman walking a dog on Desoto. Roy ran across to her and said, "Excuse me, lady, but there's a dead guy lying on the sidewalk over there."

He pointed to the northwest corner and the woman looked over.

"He's probably passed out drunk," she said. "Another Irishman who can't hold his Jameson's."

"He's not breathing," said Roy. "I'm on my way to school. I'm in the third grade at Torquemada. Maybe you should call the cops."

"They're all Irish, too," said the woman. "Who isn't in this neighborhood except for the Polacks on Rockwell."

The dog, a black cocker spaniel, began barking.

"Yes, Clancy, darlin', we'll be gettin' on now. He's hungry as a beggar in Belfast. I haven't fed him yet. You hurry, boy, you don't want to be late."

A cold wind hit them. Roy saw Clancy shiver.

"Are you going to call the cops?"

"After I feed Clancy, if I've a mind to."

She walked away.

When Roy got to school he told his friend Jimmy Boyle about the dead body.

"Most likely he ain't dead," said Jimmy, "just pissed and passed out on patrol last night tryin' to find his house. Does he look familiar?"

Dead body on DeSoto Street

"No."

"That happened to my uncle Sean a couple times when he lived with us."

"I kicked him but he didn't move."

The school bell rang.

"Do you think I should tell Mrs. McCarthy about him?"

"Nah, don't bother, she's Irish, too. When she was still Miss Kelly she used to go around with Sean until she met Frank McCarthy and married him."

Later that morning, during recess, Wendy Wicklow, Roy's friend Winky's sister, who was in the fourth grade, came up to Roy and said, "I heard you saw a dead man lying in the street with a bullet hole in his forehead."

"I saw a dead body but he didn't have a bullet hole in his forehead. Who told you that?"

"I don't know, one of the kids, everybody's talkin' about it, that it was a Polish guy. Billy O'Brian says that's how the Dublin Boyos, the gang from Bridgeport, executes people. They call a bullet between the eyes an Irish Kiss."

The Bravest Boy in the World

Roy's fourth-grade teacher, Mr. Brown, asked his class what person, living or dead, they would like to be other than themselves. Jimmy Boyle raised his hand first.

"General Custer," he said. "He was a great soldier and Indian fighter who didn't always follow orders and did things his own way until his Seventh Cavalry was way outnumbered at the Little Big Horn when a bunch of different tribes teamed up and killed Custer and all of his men. Other than that he did okay."

Bitsy DiPena raised her hand and said, "Marilyn Monroe. She's the most beautiful and popular movie star and I'm blonde, too. She can get any man she wants to marry her."

Roy raised his hand and said, "Sabu."

Mr. Brown asked, "Who is Sabu?"

"A kid from India who's an actor. He can ride elephants and wild horses and fight tigers and leopards with his bare hands and only a knife. He was in *The Thief of Baghdad*, *Elephant Boy*, *Jungle Boy* and *Cobra Woman*. He's a little guy, too, who only wears a diaper and a turban and goes barefoot. Sabu's the bravest boy in the world."

After class, Valentina Randàgia, whose family had only recently moved to Chicago, stopped Roy in the hallway and said, "Tell me about the cobra girl. I've always wanted to be a snake or have the power to change into one."

Roy had not spoken to Valentina before, nor really looked closely at her. She was a little taller than Roy, had long black hair and small green eyes.

"There's twin girls on an island, one's good and one's bad. The evil twin can turn herself into a cobra when she wants to murder someone. She's jealous of the good sister who's engaged to marry a handsome white guy. Sabu plays his sidekick, Kado. The actor who played the Wolfman is in the movie, too. Why do you want to be a snake?"

"To crawl around under people where they can't see me. That way I can sneak up on boys and bite them."

"Just boys, or girls, too?"

"Girls don't interest me, it's boys I want to bite."

The bell for the next class rang. Valentina didn't move. She kept staring into Roy's eyes.

Valentina
Randàgia

"Where did you live before coming here?"

"New Jersey."

"What does your father do?"

"I don't know him. He ran away before I was born. My mother and my Aunt Eugenia, who lives with us, are fortune-tellers, they're sisters. Eugenia was a famous burlesque performer in Newark called La Trafitta before she got too old. Trafitta means stab wound in Italian. Would you like to come over to my house?"

"Which sister is the evil one, your mother or your aunt?"

Valentina did not answer Roy's question. Her eyes were even greener now and tinier.

"Have you bitten many boys?"

"You won't come to my house, will you?"

The hallway was empty. Valentina turned around and walked away.

When Jimmy and Roy were walking home from school, Jimmy said, "I saw you talkin' to that new girl. She's different lookin', not pretty exactly but she gets me goin' a little. You like her?"

"I don't think I'm the right boy for her."

"Oh, yeah? Who is?"

"Maybe Sabu."

White Roses

Kitty had a date with Johnny Campo, their third, but she was unsure about keeping it. He would expect more from her, that she knew. Not that he wasn't attractive, in a heavy-lidded, he-mannish way, and personable, as well as being the owner of a Cadillac dealership on Clark Street, but something was missing for her. Perhaps he'd been too respectful. Kitty didn't know what to do. When she'd asked him about his name and said she had never before known anyone named Campo, he told her that it originally had been Camposanto, cemetery in Italian.

"My father changed it after his father died. He was superstitious, thought it might be bad luck. I was a little boy then, just beginning grammar school, and didn't want some other Sicilian immigrant's kid to call me Graveyard Johnny, to make fun of me. He also changed the spelling of my first name from Gianni to John. 'Sicily is where mafiosi come from,' my dad said. 'We're Americans now.'"

Kitty did not tell him that her ex-husband, Rudy, had many friends and business associates who were immigrants from Sicily and other parts of Italy. After Rudy died, two years before, several of those men and their wives had been very kind and generous to her. She and Rudy's son, Roy, who was only five at the time, they assured her, would always be part of their families; Kitty could come to them for anything they needed, including money.

Jocko Mosca was especially forthcoming. He was supposedly the boss of the organized crime syndicate in Chicago, but when she had asked Rudy about this he laughed and said, "Lies like that sell newspapers. Jocko is a businessman. He does things in unconventional ways sometimes and he's well off because of it. It's his competitors who are envious of his success, so they spread rumors, bad mouth him and try to horn in on his territory." Kitty remembered that Jocko's family was from Sicily and that his real first name was Giacomo.

She decided to call Johnny and tell him Roy wasn't feeling well, that she didn't feel comfortable leaving him with a babysitter. Before she could call, the doorbell rang. Kitty opened the front door and Johnny Campo was standing there, holding a long, narrow box.

"Hi, doll, I'm early, I know, but I got us a reservation at DeLisa's for dinner and the first show. Nat 'King' Cole is appearing tonight. You know how difficult it is to get in there but a buddy of mine and his wife can't make it so he gave us his spot. These are for you."

Campo held the box out toward Kitty.

"They're roses, white ones. I know how much you like them."

Kitty took the box.

"Look, Johnny, I can't go. I was just going to phone you. Roy's sick. June DeLisa is a good friend of mine, we can go another time."

She could see behind him snow beginning to fall.

"Well, can I come in?"

"No, Johnny, I don't want you to catch Roy's cold. It could be the flu, he's running a temperature. After calling you I was going to call the doctor."

"It's snowing," said Campo.

"I can see. You'd better get going before the roads get bad. I'm sorry, Johnny, really I am."

"All right, Kitty. I'll buzz you later."

"Don't. Roy might be asleep and the ringing would wake him up. I'll call you tomorrow."

Kitty pushed the door closed. She was holding the box. She realized that she hadn't thanked him for the roses and was about to open the door to do so but she hesitated and waited until she heard Johnny's car start and be driven away. Kitty opened the door and watched the snow come down in the darkness. Roy was at his friend Tommy Cunningham's house, he was going to spend the night there.

Johnny Campo

Crépuscule with Kitty

Kitty loved listening to her mother play "Autumn Leaves" on the piano. Rose sang the lyrics quietly while she played, often so softly that only she could understand the words.

"The autumn leaves/drift by my window/the autumn leaves/of red and gold. . . ."

Kitty was twenty-nine now, her mother was fifty-eight. In less than a year, Rose would die from a heart attack. Kitty would be thirty with an eight-year-old son to raise by herself. Roy's father had died when their boy was four, after which Rose had come to live with her daughter and grandson. Listening to her mother at the piano in the living room, Kitty felt the same as she had as a child, the age Roy was now, before Rose married her second husband, whom Kitty had never really gotten to know.

Kitty herself had remarried, a marriage that lasted only six months before being annulled. She was beginning to believe that marriage was not a good idea, at least not for her or her mother. Who among her friends was truly satisfied in her marriage?

Kitty sat at her dressing table and examined her face in the mirror. I should have a mask made, she thought, so that not only will people I know be unable to recognize me but I'll see them differently. Only Roy and Rose—maybe not even my mother—will know who I am. I can change my name, move to Los Angeles.

Kitty stared at herself for a long time, imagining what she could look like and wondering if disguising herself would really make a difference in her behavior, in her ability to make better decisions.

It was time to pick up Roy at his school. Kitty took a closer look at her face. She was still pretty but something that used to be there was missing. Her face was changing by itself. She wouldn't need a mask.

Crépuscule

Kitty and Kay

"Did he try with you?"

"He tries with every girl."

"And?"

"And what? Oh, no, nothing. I won't hold it against him."

"Won't?"

"I told him he could call me sometime."

"Quit, Kay. It won't go anywhere."

"Well, we're no angels."

"I have to hang up, Roy will be home from school any minute. He has a doctor's appointment."

"Anything serious?"

"No, they just have to remove the cast on his wrist and check that it's all right now."

"How did he hurt it?"

"Punched a kid in the head. It was sprained, not broken."

"Men."

"He's nine years old."

"Roy's a handsome boy, Kitty. He'll have plenty of girls."

"Forget him, Kay."

"Who? Roy?"

"You know who I mean. Here's Roy now."

"Hold on a sec. You didn't—with him, I mean."

"Kay, do what you want."

"If you had, you'd tell me, though."

Kitty hung up. Roy came into the kitchen through the back door.

"Roy, what happened to your cast?"

"Richie Gates cut it off with his pocket knife. Now I don't have to go to the doctor."

"He still needs to make sure your wrist has healed properly. Wash your hands, then we'll go."

Roy kissed her on the cheek.

"What was that for?"

"I bet there'll never be another girl who'll be as good to me as you are."

Kitty laughed. "I'm your mother."

Roy went to the sink and turned on the faucet.

"Ma, are you going to get married again?"

"I don't know, Roy. Maybe. Why do you ask?"

"You and Kay always talk about men. She gets into trouble a lot, doesn't she?"

"Not always. Do you want me to get married? If I did our life would probably change. Aren't you happy that it's just the two of us?"

Roy dried his hands with a dish towel.

"Sure I am, but I think about it sometimes. If you decided to marry someone would you ask me what I thought of the guy before you did?"

"I would. All right, let's go."

Roy felt his left wrist with his right hand. It was still swollen and decorated with residue from tape and plaster. Kitty put on her calico jacket, picked up her purse and walked out the front door, leaving it open. The telephone rang. He had the cut up pieces of his cast in his right side jacket pocket. Roy followed his mother out and closed the door behind him. Kitty had already started her car.

Rough Night in La Zurrona

"Pops, why in westerns do the good guys almost always wear white hats and the bad guys wear black hats?"

"White symbolizes good, black bad."

"In this movie Hoppy's the leader of the good guys but he's wearing a black hat and black clothes."

"Well, Roy, that's his signature outfit. Everyone on both sides can recognize him."

"What if one of his own men makes a mistake and shoots at him? It could happen when everyone's firing their guns at the same time and riders get in each other's way."

Roy, who was five years old, was watching an old black-and-white cowboy movie on TV on a Saturday morning with his grandfather.

"What does La Zurrona mean?"

"Loose woman, in Spanish."

"How did she get loose? Was she a prisoner who escaped?"

"The name of the town isn't meant to be about one woman. At least I don't think so."

"You mean there's more than one loose woman?"

"There are many loose women."

"Did you see that, Pops? Hoppy has a bullet hole in his hat! The bad guys are riding away. Do you think Hoppy knows any loose women?"

"I wouldn't be surprised if he does."

"They'll be glad to see him."

Roy's grandfather got up from his chair.

"I'm going to make some tea for myself, babe. Do you want anything from the kitchen?"

"Uh uh."

When his grandfather came back into the room ten minutes later, Roy told him, "There were a lot of people in the street when Hoppy's posse rode into town. Most of them were cheering and all the girls were trying to kiss him. Now Hoppy and his guys are in a saloon. He showed one of the girls the bullet hole in his hat. That one there with the golden curls."

"I can see."

"Are these women the loose ones?"

"You bet."

Later that afternoon Roy was with his mother in a grocery store waiting in the checkout line when he asked her, "Mom, were you ever in La Zurrona?"

"I don't think so. Where is that?"

"I'm not sure, maybe Mexico. Pops says there are lots of loose women there."

"He would know. Why did he tell you this?"

"Hopalong Cassidy and his boys rescued them from a gang of bad guys."

"Oh. What was the name of the movie?"

"*Rough Night in La Zurrona*. It was still daylight, though, when they took over the town."

"The really rough part happens after dark."

"The movie ended when everyone was celebrating in the saloon. What do you think happened at night? And if Pops knows, why didn't he tell me?"

"Come on, Roy, it's our turn. Help me put our groceries on the counter."

Somewhere Else

Roy was three years old when his father died. When he was five, Roy asked his mother if she missed him or wanted to go wherever he was.

"Of course I miss your dad," said Kitty, "but I can't go to where he is."

"Don't you think he'd like to see us?"

"I'll tell you about a dream I had soon after your father died. In the dream I went to meet him where he had parked his van next to a sidewalk. The side door was open and he was seated on one of the steps talking to some people. Several people were walking around on the sidewalk, packing up their belongings, all of them preparing to go somewhere. I didn't know any of them, only your dad. I approached him and asked if I could go with him. He was very busy talking to the other people and barely glanced at me but said brusquely, 'Get someone else to take you.' Then he turned away and didn't speak to me again. I was surprised not only by what he'd said but the way he'd said it. Your father never spoke to me in such a dismissive way. He didn't want me there, so I walked away. I went home and fell asleep. When I woke up I realized that your dad was going to wherever it is that dead people go, and so were the others with and around him on the street."

"Why wouldn't he take you with him?"

"Because I wasn't dead, it wasn't my time to go so I couldn't accompany him. He wasn't being rude to me, he was leaving and didn't need to explain."

"Did it make you sad?"

"Of course, Roy, but I understood."
"Will we ever see him again?"
"Not here, baby. We'll see him somewhere else."
"Okay, but I hope you'll remember to take me."

ROY'S FATHER

The Coolest Cats

Kitty had agreed to meet her friend June DeLisa at the Powder Box Beauty Salon on Diversey at two-thirty. She was early, it was only ten past two. Kitty heard music coming from a car parked in front of the Powder Box. She was standing on the sidewalk and began swaying side to side, her hips propelled by the sound of a man singing, "Pretty thing, pretty thing on my mind." A slow blues, crawling along down and hard. "I'm gonna find me a pretty woman and I'll be satisfied." The driver's side door was open, the car radio was on. Kitty looked in and saw a man in the driver's seat smoking a wrinkled yellow cigarette, his head leaned back, eyes closed.

"Who's that singing?" she asked the man.

He took a long drag on his cigarette, held the smoke in for several seconds before expelling it, coughed, then turned his head toward Kitty.

"Jimmy Reed, one of the coolest cats in town. You dig him?"

"I do. Does he live in Chicago?"

"He do."

June DeLisa pulled up in her white Cadillac Eldorado beside the man's green Mercury Monarch, rolled down her window, and shouted to Kitty, "I'll find a parking place and be right back."

June and the man in the Merc glanced at one another. He nodded, she smiled and drove away. By the time she returned on foot the Mercury was gone.

"Who was that guy?"

"I don't know. He had some good music on the radio."

"He was smoking marijuana," said June. "I could smell it from across the street."

"Uh huh. I took a couple puffs on a reefer once at a party. Made me sleepy. A pal of my ex-husband Rudy's, Freddie DiMarco, was a user. He's dead now, poor Freddie. His girlfriend hit him over the head with an iron. Cute boy."

"What happened to her?"

"She got off on self-defense, said he was beating her up, not for the first time. Dolly Lynch. She's married now to Tony Grinta."

"I remember him, one of Jocko Mosca's boys. Not cute."

June unclasped her shiny black purse, fished out a pack of Pall Malls and a book of matches, shook out a cig, lit it, and dropped the pack and matches back into the purse.

"Wash and set?"

Kitty nodded. "You?"

"Cut, little touch-up. Martinis after? Riccardo's?"

"Have you ever listened to Jimmy Reed?"

"Who's he?"

"One of the coolest cats in town."

June DeLisa laughed, coughed out smoke, and said, "Have you ever had a black boyfriend?"

"June, stop."

"Tell me, have you?"

"In 1951, '52, before I had Roy, I dated a couple of Latin guys. You met Johnny Maria."

"Not the same."

"What about you?"

June shook her head.

"Then how would you know?"

Kitty walked into the Powder Box.

She woke up in the middle of the night. The television set was on. An actress Kitty did not recognize was driving a car across a bridge. Rain hit the windshield. The woman pushed her hair out of her eyes with one hand and lost control of the steering wheel. The car smashed into the guardrail and fell off the bridge. As it plunged into the water the words The End appeared on the screen.

Kitty got up from the couch, turned off the television, and went to check on her son, Roy, in his room. He was sound asleep. Kitty walked back into the living room, turned on a lamp, and sat down on the couch. That's me, she thought, driving a car alone on a bridge in a storm. What was it June said to me today when she dropped me off? You're too hard on yourself, Kitty. What did she mean by too hard? Kitty turned off the lamp and sat still in the dark. I wouldn't have driven off the bridge, she thought. I wouldn't.

Kitty and June

Wupa: A Love Story

Whenever the actress Donatella Lampo was in Chicago, usually on a stopover between New York and Los Angeles, she made sure to visit Rudy at his place of business, Lake Shore Liquors and Pharmacy on the corner of Rush Street and Chicago Avenue in the heart of the city's nightclub district. Donatella disliked the monotony of travelling straight through the 3,000 miles between coasts by train—she refused to fly—and was always relieved to break up the trip by staying two or three days in America's second city, as it was popularly called in the 1940s and '50s.

Donatella Lampo, who had been born in a small village in Calabria, Italy, emigrated with her parents to the United States when she was four years old. The family settled on the lower East side of Manhattan, in New York City, and Donatella grew up there. Her two brothers, Pietro and Francesco, were born in New York, where they were called Peter and Frank. Donatella resisted the anglicization of her name to Donna, insisting always that she be addressed by her given Christian name. By the age of six she was acting in plays in local theater productions, and at eight was attending drama school on scholarship at the prestigious Ellen Beaumont Children's Acting Academy in midtown. Before she was twelve, Donatella was in Los Angeles, where she lived with her mother, Florentina, under contract to Metro-Goldwyn-Mayer. Her father, Carlo, a butcher, and her brothers remained in New York.

Donatella first gained international fame in the movies portraying the daughter of Vanoosh, the Vanishing Wild Man of the

Tasmanian jungle, and his mate, Tanooka. Donatella's character's name in the five Vanoosh films in which she appeared was Wupa, the Wild Child, who was most often accompanied during her meanderings through the forests by a small pack of Tasmanian dwarf tigers. Even after Donatella matured and acted in adult dramas and comedies, many of her fans referred to her as Wupa, which she never minded.

"Donatella Lampo may have gone her own way," she liked to say, "but Wupa will never be forgotten."

In Chicago, the actress usually stayed at the Moorish-styled Edgewater Beach Hotel, overlooking Lake Michigan, where she was ensconced in the personalized Wupa Rooftop Suite. One of her first stops in the city was at Lake Shore Liquors and Pharmacy, where Rudy supplied her with cosmetics and champagne, along with whatever narcotics she favored at the moment. Rudy advised her how to use the drugs in modest doses so as not to endanger her well-being, to take only enough to keep her "gliding," as Donatella described her preferred plane of consciousness.

When he was a boy, Rudy's son, Roy, had a crush on Donatella, and Rudy made sure to bring him to the store to see her. The actress always fussed over Roy and sat with him at Big Louise's lunch counter, where they sipped chocolate sodas and exchanged stories. She enjoyed hearing about Roy's baseball games and Donatella entertained him with tales of her Hollywood adventures.

"You know, Rudy," she told Roy's father, "your son is an unusual person. He's a child but he already possesses an understanding of human behavior that astounds me. If you and your wife Eva ever want to get rid of him, send him to me."

When Roy learned of the actress's untimely and shocking demise in a car wreck, he was deeply saddened. Rudy repeated to Roy Donatella's offer to have him live with her.

"How did it happen, Dad?"

"She was driving her Cadillac convertible on a hill above Malibu, lost control taking a curve too fast and went over a cliff."

He showed Roy a headline in the newspaper that read, "Wupa Perishes in Suicide Smash-Up!"

"She did it on purpose?"

"It says in the paper that Donatella left a note saying she was 'going to vanish like Vanoosh.'"

"She never got married, did she, Dad?"

"Not that I know of."

"The last time I saw Donatella she said she was going to wait for me to grow up."

Tasmanian Dwarf Tiger

Wupa
the Wild Child

The Devolution of the Snout Turner

Roy's second cousin by marriage, Wilbur Baruffa, was a television repairman. Wilbur was thirty-eight years old when he electrocuted himself and dropped dead on the spot in the back room of his garage repair shop in an alley between Topeka and Door Streets on Chicago's West Side. Roy was fourteen at the time and his mother insisted, out of respect and affection for her cousin Gertrude, Wilbur's widow, that Roy accompany her to the funeral. Roy had not exactly disliked Wilbur but neither had he enjoyed being around him during those few family gatherings Roy could not avoid attending.

Cousin Wilbur liked to corner Roy and other kids and tell them about his inventions, many of which, Wilbur was convinced, would soon be available to the public and earn him millions of dollars. One of his inventions was a fur and hide removal machine that would, Wilbur assured his listeners, expedite meat processing the world over. He had applied for a patent that had not yet been granted but he was already in negotiations, he claimed, with big companies such as Armour and Swift. The Evenizer, as Wilbur called his machine, would revolutionize the meatpacking business and put him on the cover of *Time* magazine. The Evenizer, along with a device a friend of his who supervised the hog pens at the Stockyards was experimenting with that Wilbur called the Snout Turner, were certain to secure his and Gertrude's financial future.

Wilbur wore thick spectacles, he was short, stocky, and almost completely bald. He always wore a navy blue Eisenhower jacket with "Wilbur" sewn in gold thread over the left breast pocket.

Wilbur was a constant explainer. If you were in his and Gertrude's house he would guide you to the electrical sockets in their living room and dining room and explain how he had rewired or recircuited the original system in order to amplify the capacity of each. If you were unfortunate enough to be confined in his car with him he would explain how he had tinkered with the engine or the windshield wipers to improve their efficiency, some modification the manufacturer had not provided. It was the world according to Wilbur, who considered himself a genius, and his explanations, while informative, were anything but compelling. On the contrary, they were tedious and self-congratulatory; his manner was not merely tendentious, it bordered on fiendish.

Gertrude, however, was a kind, sweet-natured, patient person. Roy liked her and did not understand how she could have subjected herself to a lifetime with a mean bore like Wilbur. Roy had witnessed his meanness, as well. Wilbur had a short temper and once, in Roy's presence, instantly became furious at the husband of a friend of Gertrude's when the man dared to contradict Wilbur on a point during one of his explanations. Roy could not remember, if he even knew, what the disagreement had been about, only that Wilbur picked up a table lamp and was about to bring it down over the other man's head when Roy's Uncle Buck, his mother's brother, stepped in and wrested the lamp away from him.

Wilbur wound up in jail after an incident that took place in public. He and Gertrude were at a restaurant in Racine, Wisconsin, where they had stopped on a Sunday afternoon, having driven up from Chicago. Wilbur liked to drive, to drive fast, often going in excess of eighty miles per hour on narrow two-lane country roads, passing or attempting to pass every vehicle ahead of him. Gertrude rarely complained to her husband about his risky driving habits, afraid that he would lose his temper and further endanger them. She mostly stared out of her passenger side window and hoped for the best.

At Gus and Essie's Fine Country Dining in Racine, Wilbur was describing for his wife how a manufacturer had tried to renege on a contract, speaking louder and louder as he explained his having outwitted the miscreant and forced him to honor the commitment. A couple at a nearby table, an elderly man and his wife, were disturbed by Wilbur's diatribe, so the man came over and asked Wilbur to please lower his voice. At first he did not comprehend what the man was requesting but when the older man persisted, Wilbur pushed him away. The man fell down and his wife left her chair and rushed to help him, as did a waitress who had been standing close by taking an order. Gertrude, also, stood up and came to the aid of the fallen man.

"Gertrude, get away!" shouted Wilbur.

When his wife failed to obey Wilbur's order, he got up and grabbed one of her arms, twisting it violently. The waitress shoved Wilbur and he punched her in the face. Two local policemen who were dining in the restaurant came over, handcuffed Wilbur, and took him into custody. They marched him out of the restaurant and deposited him in the back seat of their patrol car. Gertrude attempted to stop them and explain the situation but one of them told her they had seen everything as it happened and to meet them at the station house, then drove away.

Since Wilbur was from out of state, he was ineligible for bail on a charge of felony assault. Gertrude hired a lawyer the next day who managed to get the charge reduced to disturbing the peace, a misdemeanor, and after Gertrude paid a substantial fine Wilbur was released. Gertrude thanked the judge for his understanding and he said, "I understand they got restaurants in Illinois, lady. Eat there."

The elderly man whom Wilbur had knocked down was not seriously injured; thanks to Gertrude's repeated apologies and offer to pay for any medical expenses, he did not sue for damages, nor did the waitress, with whom Gertrude made a private financial settlement. Along with his advice to Wilbur and Gertrude to avoid dining in Wisconsin, the judge suggested that Wilbur seek counselling to control his anger.

When Gertrude told Wilbur she thought that was a good idea, Wilbur said, "That old fool interrupted me. He should have known better."

When he learned that Wilbur Baruffa had died due to self-inflicted electrocution, Roy asked his mother if she thought that he had been insane, and she said, "Everyone is at least a little bit insane, Roy. It's just that in Wilbur's case it showed."

"What about his inventions, the Evenizer and the Snout Turner? Did he ever make any money off of them?"

"I doubt it. Gertrude told me that was a terrible disappointment for Wilbur, a profound humiliation that his brilliance went unacknowledged and unrewarded. He didn't want to be remembered as just a television repairman."

"I hate to say this, Mom, but I wish I'd never met Wilbur. Maybe in a few years I won't remember him at all."

WILBUR BARUFFA

Satan's Prisoners

Roy was sixteen when he worked during the summer in a pipe-yard on Pulaski Road cutting and threading pipe. He was paired much of the time on the job with a Mexican American co-worker named Alberto Lopez, who was twenty-two. After they had been working together for a couple of weeks, Alberto asked Roy what he wanted to do with the rest of his life. Roy told him that he wanted to be a writer, that he had been writing stories since he was eleven.

"Where do you get your stories from?"

"Anywhere and everywhere. People are always telling stories, some of them are even true. If they're interesting, I write them down, others I make up."

"I've got a story for you. Want to hear it?"

"Sure."

"Danielito hooks up with a homeless woman in Mexico City named Yolanda. They're both young, in their early twenties. Yolanda is well-known on the streets in Tepito, she's like Esmeralda, the queen of the gypsies, in *The Hunchback of Notre Dame*."

"Have you read it?"

"No, but I've seen the movie. Maureen O'Hara played her, but she was Irish and didn't look like a gypsy, or like Esmeralda. Yolanda was much darker and even more beautiful than Maureen O'Hara. She had a thumbnail-size scar on her left cheek. When Danielito asked her how she got it, Yolanda became sullen and the pink mark turned crimson, her body shuddered, but she didn't explain to him how it happened, she never did.

"They went together to Bakersfield, California, to work in the fields, crossed the border illegally on February 29th, her birthday. She told him it was el día de Santa Yolanda de los prisioneros del diablo, the patron saint of Satan's prisoners, that it comes only when there's a second full moon in the month on the final day of February in a leap year, and that she was named after her. Satan's prisoners, she told Danielito, are those souls sold to Satan during the person's lifetime. People who reform before their death and attempt to undo the deal by immersing themselves in holy water die horribly when the holy water turns to flames.

"Yolanda was born in Jalisco. Her father had bargained with the devil in order to save the life of his wife, who was dying from cancer. Satan told him that his wife would be cured only if he promised also to sell him the souls of his two sons and his daughter, Yolanda, the youngest child. The father agreed and his wife lived a full life. Both of the sons died, one from a gunshot, the other in a work accident where he was run over and cut to pieces by a tractor. The man died from grief, a heart attack, soon thereafter. His daughter, Yolanda, ran away to Mexico City, where she became a whore.

"Satan wanted her to join him, to be his bride, but she beguiled him in ways even the King of Cruelty had never imagined. He said he would wait for her until her life of misery became unbearable and he could claim her. The first time she gave herself to a man for money, after it was finished, she cut herself on her perfect face with a sharp edge of a rock so she would never be beautiful again, inside or out."

"I thought you said that she never told Danielito how she got her scar."

"She didn't, she told me. Much later."

"You? Why?"

"Wait. I will tell you. In Bakersfield, Danielito began working on cars with a mechanic called The Wizard. He was a mad genius who had designed a super stock engine that he said would defeat any other car and revolutionize stock car racing. Danielito buried himself in this work and Yolanda found a job as a waitress. She also resumed her whoring but did not confess this to Danielito.

"The devil came to her in the form of a rich widow, a woman named Dolores Delmonte, who owned a cattle ranch and many oil wells. Yolanda and Dolores Delmonte became lovers, Dolores was obsessed with her and promised her money. Yolanda, however, was friends with another waitress, who told her that she should come with her to Chicago, where she had relatives and there was a large Mexican community. Yolanda learned during lovemaking with Dolores Delmonte that she had murdered her husband, Rafael, then paid off the territorial judge to declare his death was accidental. Dolores made plans to take Yolanda to Europe, from where, she said, she and Yolanda would never have to return, and gave to Yolanda the money The Wizard needed to complete his construction of La Sensación, his super car. Danielito discovers the relationship Yolanda has with the rich widow and her plans to take Yolanda away. In The Wizard's garage, in front of Yolanda and Danielito, Dolores Delmonte pulls a gun and fires it at Danielito, but Yolanda grabs her arm and the bullet hits The Wizard, wounding him. Yolanda tells Dolores that unless she leaves her and Danielito alone she will swear to a new judge that Dolores murdered Rafael and attempted to kill Danielito.

"Dolores flees and probably departs for Europe by herself. The Wizard recovers and he and Danielito finish working on La Sensación, which The Wizard has entered in a big race against the top cars and drivers in Southern California. Danielito will drive the car. Yolanda agrees to go with them to the race, saying she will drive another car and meet them at the racetrack. Instead, Yolanda drives to the bus station in Bakersfield, where she meets her waitress friend, and together they take a bus to Chicago."

"What happened to Yolanda in Chicago?"

"She was pregnant, she had a child, a boy. She worked and raised him by herself. When he was old enough she told her son the story of her life before Chicago, including how she got the scar. Soon after this, Yolanda suffered a mysterious illness, one no doctor could identify, and she died."

"The devil took her."

"Yes."

"What became of her son?"

"He does the best he can. He works now in a pipeyard in Chicago. Perhaps some day someone will tell the world his story."

ALBERTO LOPEZ

Cop Killer

"You know Dickie Keegan, the kid was expelled from St. Thespis for beatin' up the school janitor?"

"Yeah, last time I saw him was in Bucktown throwin' iceballs at passin' cars on Diversey. Said he wouldn't quit until he broke a windshield and a car went off the road."

"He killed a cop."

"You're jokin'. For what?"

"He was shakin' down younger kids for change, like he always done, a cop spotted him and tried to arrest him. Keegan grabbed the cop's gun and shot him. He's on the run now."

"Jesus, Buzzy, Keegan's seventeen. He could get the chair."

"His old man's doin' a stretch for armed robbery in Indiana. Ruby Brown told me. Her mother used to go out with his brother."

Roy and Buzzy were sitting on the back porch steps of Buzzy's house on a cold, drizzly November day. They were used to the weather. Buzzy had told Roy that his older sister, Estelle, once complained about it at dinner and asked their father why they didn't move to California, and he said, "Are you kiddin'? California's full of weirdos and phonies who got pushed out of New York and other cities back east. The broads're all tramps lookin' for suckers."

"How do you know?" Estelle said. "You've never been there. I could go to the beach every day, maybe even get into the movies."

"Right, you'd be a tramp in no time."

"Where do you think Keegan'll go?" Roy asked Buzzy. "I doubt that he's ever been out of Chicago."

"If I was him, I'd try to leave the country. Mexico, get lost down there."

"I'll bet he'll get caught right here, Buzz. He's a cop killer. They won't quit until they find him."

Two days later, Dickie Keegan was captured at the Greyhound Bus terminal. In his pockets were the gun he'd taken from the cop he'd murdered, twenty-five bucks, and a ticket to San Diego, California. The day after police nabbed him, Roy's mother told him that she'd read about it in the *Tribune*.

"Ed Keegan's son," she said. "His father was a bad penny in the old days."

"Did you know him?"

"Your father did. We used to run into him in the clubs. He always had a heat on."

"Buzzy Hermanski says Dickie's dad is in prison in Indiana."

"Doesn't surprise me. Your dad finally had to eighty-six him from the liquor store. Keegan was a mean drunk, scared the customers. Your father would give him a fifth of rye off the shelf and send him on his way."

"Dad knew how to handle people."

"He was usually gentle, and generous. He'd slip a couple of bucks to the neighborhood rummies and old people who lived around the store. If someone got out of hand, he or Uncle Lou or one for the beat cops who came in took care of business. Too bad about the Keegan kid, though. I'm sure he had a hard home life. I heard his mother was a cripple, I think from polio. I never met her."

"What if I did something crazy like kill a cop or somebody? Would you help me? I mean, give me money and ask one of Dad's connections to smuggle me out of town?"

"I won't even answer that question, Roy. You'd never do anything so stupid. You're fifteen, you know how to stay out of trouble."

"What if Dad were alive? What would he do?"

Roy's mother looked at him crosseyed, then said, "He'd say to me, 'Kitty, I'll do what I can to fix it, but however it goes, kiss Roy goodbye.'"

"I got it, Ma, I won't ask you any more questions."

Dickie Keegan

Kidnapped (Ancòra)

"What is it exactly that's disturbing you now, Kitty? Have you been taking the pills I prescribed?"

Kitty straightened up in her chair and threw her shoulders back the way she always told her son, Roy, to do.

"I take them, but not all the time. They make me sleepy."

"I thought that's what you wanted them for, to help you sleep."

"I'm afraid of my dreams, doctor, they're not good."

"What happens in them?"

"I don't know, they're confusing. The most common one is when someone, usually a woman, is trying to kidnap my son."

"How old is Roy?"

"Five and a half."

"Has anyone ever threatened to kidnap him?"

Kitty shook her head. "Of course not. That's just it, it doesn't make sense, does it?"

"It depends. Dreams don't necessarily make sense, they don't need to. I'd say it's not unusual for you to feel protective of him, especially since your divorce. How often does he see his father?"

"Once a week, on Saturdays, when Rudy's in town."

"Do they get along all right?"

"Absolutely, Roy and he are very close. They talk on the phone several times during the week. Rudy's extremely generous with his support for both Roy and myself."

"You and he are on good terms?"

Kitty nodded. "We're friends. We want the best for Roy. Rudy's remarried now."

Kitty's
doctor

"Do you recognize any of the women in your dreams who are trying to steal Roy away from you?"

"None of them is Rudy's wife, if that's who you mean. She's a good person, I like her."

"How old are you, Kitty?"

"Twenty-eight. I'll be twenty-nine in November."

"Is your mother still living with you?"

"Uh uh, she went back to Florida. Chicago is too cold for her."

"Does she ever appear in your dreams?"

Kitty closed her eyes and did not answer right away. When she opened her eyes she said, "Only once that I can remember. I was in the dream, too. I was a girl, ten or eleven years old, wearing a pretty dress, white with puffy sleeves that covered the eczema sores on my arms. A man was coming to visit us at our house and my mother wanted me to look nice for him."

"Was it your father?"

"I don't think so. She said his name, I didn't know him."

"Were you afraid this man was coming to take you away?"

Kitty stood up.

"Can you give me some different pills?"

"Why don't you just stop completely taking the ones you have and let's see what happens."

Kitty threw back her shoulders. The doctor's face was blurry.

"Does talking like this help your other patients? Women, I mean."

"Sometimes. Everyone is different."

Kitty was sitting in her car when she began to cry. She rested her head on the top of the steering wheel before suddenly sitting up straight. She looked at her face in the rear view mirror. The whites of her eyes were grey. She would be thirty in November, not twenty-nine.

No Telling

"Do you remember the scene at the end of that movie we watched on tv in my hotel room, *Treasure of the Sierra Madre*, where the old man and one of the other guys he'd been working a gold mine with up in the mountains are riding horses with a bunch of Mexicans into a desert windstorm to try to recover the gold dust they'd left behind in small canvas sacks?"

"Yeah. Bandits who'd stolen the pack mules from their partner, then killed him, hadn't known those sacks contained gold and cut them loose from where they'd been tied onto the backs of the mules and now the wind was blowing the dust into their faces."

"That's what it felt like when your mother threw my clothes and other belongings out of her bedroom window at me when I went to the house the last time."

Roy, who was eleven years old, was being driven by his mother's second ex-husband, Harry, to the private hospital she was staying in.

"How long do you think she'll have to be there?"

"Her friend June said Kitty's doctor told her a month, maybe more. There's no telling with a nervous breakdown."

The hospital was in a suburb of Chicago Roy had never been to.

"How much farther is it?"

"We'll be there in forty-five minutes, if there's not too much traffic. Did you tell the McLaughlins that you were going with me to see your mother?"

"No. I have a key to their house."

They rode for a while without talking, then Roy asked, "Do you think my mother is really crazy?"

"I can't answer that question, Roy."

"Can't or don't want to?"

"Both."

Harry drove faster.

Harry

A Quart of Milk for Mother

"Roy, here's fifty cents. Run down to Selma's Grocery and get a quart of milk."

Roy, who was nine years old, took two quarters from his mother and put on his navy tanker jacket.

"It's snowing, take a hat."

He took his black Chicago White Sox cap and left the house. Roy walked half a block and then cut through the alley behind Ojibway Boulevard. Snow was already ankle deep, it felt soft under Roy's gym shoes. A tramp was bent over a large rusty garbage can behind Buddy Logan's house, digging through it and tossing junk onto the ground. Roy stopped a few feet away and watched. After about a minute the tramp picked up the can, turned it over and dumped out what was left in it. The tramp had long, scraggly gray and black hair and was wearing a brown-stained green GI jacket. It took Roy another thirty seconds to realize that the tramp was a woman. Her baggy black pants were ripped open at both knees.

"What're you lookin' for?" Roy asked.

The woman did not answer or look at him. She knelt down on her bare knees and sorted through the trash. Roy moved closer to the woman and looked at her face. Her right cheek had a gash in it that was crusted over with dried blood. Despite her gray hair she had a fairly young face. Roy thought she might be about the same age as his mother, who was thirty-two. The woman put a couple of things Roy could not identify into her coat pockets and stood up. She was not very much taller than Roy. She turned and stared at him with her mouth half open, enough for him to see that most of her front teeth were missing. He was surprised to see how bright her blue eyes were. Roy dug into his right front pants pocket and took out one of the quarters his mother had given him. He held it out toward the woman.

"This is almost all I've got," he said.

She reached out the filthy fingers of her right hand and daintily accepted it. The silver coin shone like a moon on the

Woman in the alley

tips of her thumb, index and middle fingers. She deposited the quarter in one of her pockets and slowly began walking away from Roy down the alley. Suddenly he ran after her and put his White Sox cap on her head. She did not turn to look at him. The snow was falling harder.

At Selma's Roy took a quart-sized bottle of milk from the refrigerator, brought it to the counter and handed the other quarter to Selma.

"Can I bring you twenty-five cents later?" Roy asked her. "I gave one of the quarters my mother gave me to a bum in the alley."

"Sure, Roy. I know you're good for it."

"The bum was a woman."

"Yes, dear. Tell your mother hello."

Roy walked back through the alley. The trash the woman had dumped out of the Logans' garbage can was almost completely concealed under the snow. Roy thought that she had to be pretty strong to have lifted up the can the way she did.

When he got home, his mother saw that his hair was wet.

"Didn't you wear a hat?" she said.

"A big kid I never saw before stole it from me and he robbed me, too. We owe Selma a quarter."

To Beat the Devil

After Roy's grandfather, whom he called Pops, died, Roy's mother's brother, Buck, came north from Florida to Chicago to bury the body. This was in February of 1960, two-day-old dirty snow was piled against the curbs and sidewalks were coated with ice. Pops had been living in a Florida nursing home for a few months prior to his fatal heart attack. Buck had moved his father to Tampa, where he lived with his wife and daughter, with the intention of having Pops live with them, away from the cold weather, but it had been necessary to instead place Pops in an assisted living facility where he could have on-site medical care. Pops had not wanted to leave Chicago, his home for sixty years, but he and his daughter did not get along, so Roy's uncle assumed responsibility for him.

Following his grandfather's funeral and burial, Roy, who was fourteen, accompanied his uncle around Chicago to say hello to former business associates of Buck's and to visit neighborhoods in which his uncle had built houses. Buck was a civil engineer and architect. He had relocated to Tampa two years before where there were more opportunities and fewer building restrictions. He also preferred being in warm weather year-round.

After cruising through the city and adjoining suburbs, Buck parked the car he'd borrowed from his sister in front of a one-story flat-roofed building with a sign on it that read DOMBROSKI & SON MACHINERY AND MANUFACTURING. It was only two-thirty in the afternoon but the sky was already dark and cloudy, threatening snow.

"Why are you stopping here, Unk?"

"There's a guy I want to see."

"Dombroski?"

"When I left Chicago he owed me some money. I heard he died. Maybe I can collect from his son."

"A lot of money?"

"Enough to give it a try."

"Can I come in with you? It'll be cold in the car."

"I'll leave the engine running with the heater on. This shouldn't take long."

Buck got out of the car and entered the building. Roy turned on the radio and listened to the news. Workers at a factory on the south side were on strike and someone got stabbed. The cops arrested two of the strikers and the victim was taken away in an ambulance. The White Sox had traded Chico Carrasquel, their shortstop, to the Cleveland Indians in order to make room for a top prospect, Luís Aparicio. Both players were from Venezuela. Snow was expected to begin falling on the city by four o'clock and continue throughout the night. People were advised to do their grocery shopping early, before the snow accumulated and made getting around difficult.

Roy turned off the radio. Flurries landed on the windshield. Roy had to pee, so he cut the ignition, put the key in a coat pocket, got out of the car, and ran around one side of the Dombroski building into the alley behind it. He urinated against the back wall, hoping nobody would see him. After Roy finished, he hurried back to the car. His uncle was standing next to the driver's side door. Buck's curly black hair was littered with white flakes.

"Sorry, Unk. I needed to pee bad."

He handed the car key to Buck.

"Did Dombroski's kid fork over what his old man owed?"

"Get in the car and I'll tell you."

Buck didn't say anything until he'd driven a couple of blocks. He turned on the windshield wipers.

"Turns out Dombroski was murdered a year ago. The business was in debt. His son, Buddy, declared bankruptcy. He gave me the phone number of the lawyer who's handling the claims. It doesn't matter, though, because his father and I never drew up a paper, it was a private matter."

"Who murdered him? Someone else he owed money to?"

"Buddy thinks the killer was the husband of a girl Dombroski was playing around with on the side."

"Is the husband in jail?"

"No. They can't prove he did it."

Snow was coming down harder, earlier than they said on the radio it would.

"Women and money, Roy, a man can't do without them, but there's always hell to pay."

"I once heard Pops say, 'Nobody beats the devil.' Is that what you mean?"

The snow came at them now from different angles, evading the swiping blades, clinging to the windshield.

"All I know, Roy, is that living is a very dangerous business."

DOMBROSKI

Big Hands

Midafternoon, late August, Roy and his friend Jimmy Boyle had just finished playing a baseball game at Heart-of-Jesus park. Both boys were eleven years old. They were sitting on a bench alongside the field taking off their spikes and putting on their street shoes when a small man neither of them had ever seen before sat down on the bench. He was wearing a gray hat, a shabby blue sport coat, and a brown-stained yellow tie. He needed a shave. His long, slightly bent nose was pockmarked, as were his pale cheeks. He watched as the boys tied the laces of their spikes together in order to carry them over a shoulder.

"I used to do that, too," said the man. "We all did."

Roy and Jimmy looked at him briefly, then turned away.

"Of course that was a very long time ago, more than fifty years. I'm fifty-five now, same as this century. In 1921 I pitched and sometimes played second base for the Orphans, the Hebrew Orphan Asylum in New York City. I grew up there, on the Lower East Side, Second Street. Everybody in the neighborhood knew me, Nappy Buchinsky. I came here to Chicago before the last war, worked on tugboats on the Great Lakes with my friend Harmon Wieseltier. His uncle Phil was in the business. Harmon drowned in 1932, in the St. Lawrence Seaway. His body was never recovered, current took it. I quit the tugs after that, worked in a sausage factory—though I never have ate pig in my life—then begun runnin' errands for The Outfit. Still do. I like to come to the park here, watch the games.

"You handle yourself pretty good at shortstop," he said to Roy.

"Where'd you learn to backhand grounders to your right instead of tryin' to front the ball? What's your name? Mine's Nappy, short for Napoleon, what the other kids called me 'cause I was always givin' orders."

"Watchin' Chico Carrasquel, the White Sox shortstop. I'm Roy, this is Jimmy, he plays centerfield."

"You boys have families?"

"Yeah. Why?"

Nappy Buchinsky
Pitcher Hebrew Orphans
1921

HEBREW ORPHAN ASYLUM

Hebrew Orphan Asylum baseball team 1920

"I was raised in an orphanage. My mother, father, and sister, Esther, were killed in a pogrom in Poland. Esther was nine, I was five, when it happened. People from our village hid me and later got me on a boat to America."

"What's a pogrom?" asked Roy.

"Soldiers would murder the Jews. You boys Jewish?"

"Roy's father was."

"He died when I was four."

"You still got your mother, though, yes?"

Roy nodded.

"In the Orphan Asylum were kids whose families were slaughtered in Russia, Poland, and Germany, just because they were Jews."

"My mother's Catholic, when she was a girl she went to boarding school at Our Lady of Divine Inspiration in Indiana. Jimmy's parents are from Ireland."

"I don't think there's pogroms in America," said Jimmy. "I never heard about none."

"No, not like in the old country," Nappy said. "But lots of people here don't like Jews, either."

"Why?"

"No good reason. Maybe because the Jews consider themselves the Chosen People, a separate race. You don't have to practice Judaism to be Jewish. In the old country we were called Orientals."

Jimmy and Roy stood up. All of their teammates were gone.

"We've gotta go," said Jimmy.

"I have a question."

"Yes, Roy?"

"When you pitched for the orphanage, what was your best pitch?"

"My back-up ball."

Nappy Buchinsky took a baseball out of Roy's glove. He had big hands.

"I held it like this, not with my fingers wrapped around it, but back against the palm of my hand. I threw it same as I did a fastball but it don't go as fast. Got batters to start their swing early. If they hit it, they popped the ball up or hit a weak grounder, usually back to me so I could throw 'em out easy."

"Why didn't you play in the big leagues?" asked Jimmy.

"The majors didn't want Jews, or Negroes, either. I don't know if I coulda been good enough, anyway. But I got by in New York City. There were lots of Jews there."

While he and Jimmy were walking home, Roy held the ball in his right hand the way Nappy had.

"I couldn't control that back-up pitch," he said. "I'd need to use my fingers more, so it wouldn't work."

"Did your dad have big hands?"

"I don't remember. Why?"

"Maybe Jews got bigger hands than us."

Chinese Necklace Mystery

"Can you tell please, where is precious necklace?"

"In the top drawer of the dresser in my bedroom. I never tried to hide it."

"Honorable son, go to dresser in bedroom, find necklace, bring me."

Dr. Yee's son, Bailey, left the living room. He was gone for only thirty seconds before returning with the necklace. He held it out to his father and said, "Here it is, Pop, just as she said."

Dr. Yee looked at it.

"Put in pocket, not take out until later."

"What are you going to do with me?" asked Dahlia Li without rising from her couch.

"Dr. Yee come only for necklace, not Dahlia Li. Son Bailey Yee and difficult father leave now."

"What's difficult about you, Dr. Yee? Or do you wish that to remain a mystery?"

"Pop isn't in the habit of explaining how he figures things out. Are you, Pop?"

"Son not need understand father, only obey and observe."

"In other words, Dr. Yee, even though you are considered more brilliant a detective than Judge Dee, you're the same as any other man."

Dr. Yee took a long look at Dahlia Li before saying, "Beautiful lady misunderstand. My job over, not talk more than necessary."

Dr. Yee bowed toward her, then he and his son left the apartment. The words THE END appeared on the television screen.

Roy turned it off. He looked out the window. It was still raining. He was nine years old and wished his father were still alive.

Dr. Yee

The Swimming Lesson

In 1959, eight months after Roy's father died, his widow, Evie, Rudy's second wife, took Roy, who was eleven years old, and his brother, Mickey, who was five and a half, on a trip to New York. Roy was Rudy's son by his first wife, Kitty, and Evie was Mickey's mother. Rudy and Kitty had divorced when Roy was five. Kitty and Evie got along well, and Evie treated Roy as if he were her own son. She wanted to give the boys—and herself—a little holiday following the death of her husband at the age of forty-eight. Neither she nor the boys had been to New York, so she thought it would be a timely and educational adventure for the three of them.

Roy had previously travelled often with his mother, mostly in the southern United States, to New Orleans and Florida in particular, and to Cuba. He liked living in Chicago but was always happy to get away, to experience and explore new places. In New York City Evie took Rudy's sons to a couple of Broadway shows, to museums, and to watch the Yankees play the White Sox at Yankee Stadium. They ate in good restaurants and took long walks on the streets and through the parks in Manhattan, where they stayed in a big hotel on Fifth Avenue. Evie had grown up in Chicago, the youngest of ten children in a poor family. She was twenty-two when she married Rudy, who was a successful businessman, and they lived together happily for seven years. His premature passing had been a shock to Evie, and Rudy's older brother and sister had been unkind to her in the aftermath. Getting away from them was reason enough for going to New York.

After a few days in the city, Evie, Roy, and Mickey went north to a resort in the mountains, where they swam, went horseback riding, and went on hikes in the woods. The most fun for Roy were swimming lessons in the hotel pool, where the instructor was the former Olympic champion swimmer and movie star Buster Crabbe. Roy had seen Crabbe in his heroic roles as Tarzan, Flash Gordon, and good-guy cowboys on Saturday mornings in serials at the Nortown, Roy's neighborhood movie theater, and was thrilled to be in his presence. Crabbe told all the kids to call him Larry, his real first name. He was kind to and patient with them, especially with those who were less proficient or merely beginners. Roy was already a pretty good swimmer, having spent a considerable amount of time with Kitty swimming in the Atlantic Ocean and Gulf of Mexico. Crabbe taught Roy the butterfly and back strokes and how better to breathe underwater. Mickey learned how to dive off the side of the pool and to dog paddle without using an inner tube. Both boys had a great time with their new friend, Larry, while Evie relaxed and became acquainted with the other adult guests. She met an amiable single man named Conway, a widower in his early fifties from Detroit. Conway treated her and the boys to lunches and dinners and two or three times joined Evie for late-night drinks in the hotel lounge.

"Are you going to marry Conway and make us move to Detroit?" Mickey asked his mother.

Evie laughed and said, "I hardly know the man, of course not. Besides, we're going back to Chicago the day after tomorrow."

On their last day at the pool, Roy asked Crabbe if he would give him his autograph.

"Could you please sign it 'Buster'?" he said.

Crabbe smiled and wrote on the back of a hotel menu, "For Roy, keep working on your backstroke. Best of luck always from your pal, Larry, and from his friends Buster, Tarzan, and Flash. Don't let the girls lead you astray!"

Riding in the car taking Evie, Roy, and Mickey to the airport, Roy asked Evie the meaning of the word astray.

"Why would you ask me that?"

"Larry wrote it when he signed the menu for me. He wrote, 'Don't let the girls lead you astray.'"

Evie giggled. "He warned you not to allow anyone to make you do anything that isn't right, to not go the wrong way in life."

"Why did he say girls?"

"Well, Roy, I suppose he learned about that in Hollywood. Even Flash Gordon can sometimes make a mistake."

Larry 'Buster' Crabbe

The Romantic

"Did you ever hear of a French writer named Pierre Loti?"

"No, what did he write?"

"Many novels. A long time ago, nobody reads him anymore, I shouldn't think. He died in the early 1920s. His real name was Julien Viaud, there's a street in Paris named after him."

"Have you read his books?"

"Only one, *Fantôme d'Orient.* I tried another, *La Troisième Jeunesse de Madame Prune.* An attractive title, but I couldn't get through it. Some notable contemporary writers, such as Marcel Proust and Henry James, thought highly of him. Loti was an interesting character, bisexual, passed himself off as a Bedouin or a circus acrobat. He liked to wear costumes. For several years he was a sailor in the French navy, then had a series of adventures in Turkey and Arabia. He was enraptured by the exotic, a romantic."

Roy, who was an aspiring writer, was listening to his friend Francis Reeves, an older man, who was widely read and whose suggestions often helped guide Roy's efforts at self-education.

"What do writers do if they fall out of fashion and the public stop buying their books?"

Francis laughed. "They either get a job or commit suicide."

Roy was in New York City visiting his friend Rusty James, with whom he had gone to high school in Chicago. Rusty was a painter who was having a great early success selling his work. Both he and Roy were twenty-three years old. Roy repeated to Rusty what Francis had said about a writer losing his audience.

"It could happen to any artist," Rusty said. "That's why I'm saving the money I'm making now."

"Francis told me about a French novelist in the last century who had been very popular then fallen into relative obscurity and become a Muslim who called himself The Pasha."

"Some people are better at fooling themselves than others. I'd rather just go to work as a railroad brakeman."

Roy did not feel the need to disguise himself other than to create a fictional persona. Perhaps as part of his self-examination into his own identity, sexual and otherwise, Loti took fictional exploration a step further, indulging a desire to act out these inventions, a way to codify or verify his findings. This dramatization and role-playing may have determined Loti's direction, both as a writer and an individual.

When Roy related his speculation about the French writer to Francis Reeves, the older man replied, "Pierre Loti undoubtedly had a fecund imagination, embodying no end of viable impersonations. After all, he lived for a very long time."

"He definitely had a great gift for invention," Roy said.

"Yes," said Francis. "Pity it didn't make him a greater writer."

Pierre Loti

Bring Me the Head of Mangas Coloradas

"What are you watching, Roy?"

"An old western movie, *Shootout at Dead Indian*."

Roy's grandfather sat down in a chair next to where Roy was sitting on the floor.

"What a terrible title," he said.

"What's so terrible about it, Pops?"

"The name of wherever that place is. The United States Army slaughtered the indigenous people on this continent for centuries to make way for emigrants from Europe. Christopher Columbus called them Indians because he thought he'd arrived in India. And later, archaeologists theorized that they originally came from Asia."

"Did they?"

"At one time the North American and Asian continents were connected by a land bridge over the Bering Strait. The theory is that people from Asia, Mongolians, mostly, walked across to what is now named Alaska, then gradually moved south to where the weather was warmer, though some remained in the north. The ones who came to inhabit the southwest are called Anasazi in the Navajo language, which means Ancient Warriors. The Europeans came later and did their best to wipe them out. They still are."

"You're from Europe."

"Yes, Roy. I was a boy when I came here, like you are now. I didn't have a choice."

"How do you know so much about this?"

"I read."

"Is it true that white men took scalps like the Indians did?"

"Some did, as a kind of revenge, to show the Indians that they could be just as savage and disrespectful of their culture and religious beliefs. Not only did the whites take scalps, they also beheaded Indian leaders such as Osceola of the Seminoles and Mangas Coloradas of the Chiricahua Apaches, who was shot, scalped and decapitated. Supposedly his head was given to the Smithsonian Museum in Washington, D.C., to be displayed, but it never was. The museum curators claimed it was lost, but most likely it was sold to a private collector. That happened in 1863, almost a hundred years ago."

Mangas Coloradas

"In this movie one of the white men helps captured Indians get away before the killers can hang them for stealing horses that belonged to the Indians in the first place. Then he falls in love with an Indian woman and marries her."

"Did they go to live somewhere else?"

"No. Her brother, who's the leader of a renegade band, murders her for betraying their race."

"There are bad people of all races, Roy, just as there are good ones. My advice is to deal with people as individuals, make up your own mind who's worth your time."

"What turns people bad, Pops?"

"Fear. They're afraid and don't even know it."

"Good people get frightened, too."

"That's true, Roy, but some people can handle it better than others."

"Can you handle it, Pops?"

"Not always. That's what's wrong with the world. Sometimes it's difficult to do the right thing, or even to figure out what the right thing is."

Roy turned off the television set.

"Don't you want to see how the movie ends?"

"I think I know."

Life Is Like This Sometimes

Roy rode the train from Oakland, California, to Ogden, Utah, where he arrived at Sunday midnight. From there he had to catch a bus to Logan, to meet a friend. The next one was not scheduled to depart until six a.m., so Roy had several hours to kill in Ogden, a town he did not know.

It was late November, very cold, snow and ice on the ground. Roy walked into a bar full of Indians. The name of the place was Dot's Hot Spot. He took a stool and ordered a beer from the bartender, who resembled a retired Irish cop from Chicago Roy used to talk to at the racetrack named Eddie Dooley. Dooley had been forced to retire after the horse he'd been riding down State Street during a Saint Patrick's Day parade had collapsed from a heart attack, fallen on Eddie, and crushed his right leg. One day at Sportsman's he told Roy he was now "takin' it out on the ponies." The last Roy heard of Eddie he was repairing refrigerators.

Dot's Hot Spot stayed open all night and was full of Indians who were either already drunk or about to be. During the course of the night several men slid off their stools and collapsed to the floor, where they remained undisturbed until they woke up and again took a place at the bar. The popular belief among white men was that Indians could not hold their liquor particularly well. From what Roy had observed by that time—he was twenty-one—neither could most white men.

Roy sipped his beer, listened to Charlie Rich and Freddie Fender on the Rock-Ola, and kept an eye out for trouble that might be headed his way. Roy didn't want trouble, he just wanted to get to

Logan. A white man with red hair cut short who looked to be about forty-five years old came in and sat down on the stool to Roy's left. He ordered a shot of bar whiskey and a beer. He nodded at Roy.

"Looks like we're in the minority," he said.

"Oh, I don't know," said Roy. "I think most of these boys are drinking about the same as us."

"You got a point, hotshot," the man said.

They talked for a while. His name was Rigney. Roy never asked if it was his first, last, or only. He told Roy he had been up to Draper to visit his sister, who was doing a dime for armed robbery.

"She knocked down a couple or three laundromats, along with her boyfriend, Walter Topper. He put Rita up to it. Hotshot jumped bail, but he can't stay disappeared forever. I'd hunt Walter Topper down and take him out of the count, Rita wanted me to.

"I've met a hundred men like Topper, maybe more. So will you, probably, before you're through. Men with nothin' inside. I'm one now, I suppose. Used to I did. Hard time'll do that to anyone. Your old man ever put a pistol to your head and tell you if he pulled the trigger he'd be savin' you from a lifetime of trouble? I was eight when mine done that. He weren't wrong, just incapable of figurin' out how to fit into this earthly paradise. Hanged himself in a clothes closet twenty years ago, nineteen fifty-two. How's a boy to profit from that?"

They drank more. Rigney switched from whiskey to tequila somewhere along in there while Roy nursed a few beers. Roy wasn't much of a drinker and he did not want to risk being kept from boarding the bus because he was drunk. Roy had promised to meet his friend in Logan by nine-thirty. .

Rigney rolled up his shirtsleeves. Tattooed in large gothic letters on his left forearm was the name RUTH. A few Indians got into a tussle at the other end of the bar but it didn't travel. To Roy's relief, it was a pretty quiet night in Dot's Hot Spot. Toward morning it occurred to him to ask Rigney who Ruth was.

"I don't know anybody named Ruth," he said.

They didn't talk after that except to say goodbye and good luck. At five-thirty Roy left the bar and went to catch his bus. Two of the Indians who had been in Dot's Hot Spot staggered into the Trailways station. The taller of the two wore a calico half-Stetson and a braid halfway down his back. He was one of the men who had been involved in the brief scuffle. A cop stopped them and ordered them to go outside and come back later when they were sober. The shorter Indian, who was hatless, passed out and slumped to the ground. His partner went out the door in a hurry. The cop picked up the Indian who had collapsed under his arms and dragged him outside.

From the window of the bus as it pulled out of Ogden Roy saw Rigney walking on the side of the road. It was snowing and he didn't have a coat.

Rigney

The Tiger

Ever since Roy could remember, a tiger often appeared in his dreams. He did not know why but later in life he learned that in some cultures, mostly in Asia and Eastern Europe, the tiger is a representation of an evil spirit, even an avenging figure, at the very least a portent of danger.

The night before his eighth birthday a tiger was following him through a forest. Roy wanted to run but he did not have command of his legs. He felt the tiger close behind him, though it did not make a sound. Suddenly, Roy turned around, expecting to be devoured. He and the tiger stared at each other, then Roy woke up. It was unusually cold for mid-October in Chicago, almost freezing. Roy looked out the window next to his bed at a pitchblack sky.

Roy had difficulty getting back to sleep but when he awoke it was the day after his birthday. His mother was sitting next to him on his bed.

"Sweetheart, I've been so worried about you. You developed a fever the night before last and slept for almost a day and a half. I telephoned the parents of the children you'd invited to the party and told them it was cancelled due to your illness, but don't worry, we'll set another date and celebrate your birthday a little later. I'm just glad you're all right now. The doctor says he isn't sure what caused this to happen."

"I am," said Roy.

Mary Ann Wilson

When Kitty Colby attended boarding school at Our Lady of Everlasting Obedience in Blissful Plains, Illinois, in the late 1930s and early '40s, the only other student she felt was her real friend was Mary Ann Wilson. Kitty was from Chicago and Mary Ann was from Mississippi Falls, a small town near the Kentucky border. Kitty was extremely shy and intimidated by the strict discipline enforced by the nuns, whereas Mary Ann appeared unbothered by their harshness and occasional brutality. Both girls were the same age, tall and pretty; Kitty a brunette with dark brown eyes and Mary Ann a blonde with blue eyes.

The girls did not like being separated during the summers. They sent postcards to each other weekly and spoke on the telephone as often as possible. Kitty felt safe when Mary Ann was with her at school, protected from what she perceived as dismissive and rude behavior directed at her by other boarders. Mary Ann ignored this exclusionary attitude, floating above what she described to Kitty as "dumb girl stuff."

"We're prettier and smarter than any of them and that makes them unhappy," she told Kitty. "They're jealous, is all."

When Mary Ann got sick and had to be sent home to Mississippi Falls, she was thirteen years old. She and Kitty had been friends for five years and Kitty felt lost without her. She prayed every day for Mary Ann's recovery and begged the nuns for information as to her friend's condition. All they told her was that Mary Ann was in God's hands, whatever happened to her was up to Him.

At Kitty's request, after almost a month without news, her

mother called Mary Ann's parents and learned that she had pneumonia. Two weeks later the students were informed by their Mother Superior that Mary Ann had died.

Following her best friend's death, life for Kitty at Our Lady of Everlasting Obedience became unbearable; she suffered from depression and was eventually withdrawn by her mother from school for the remainder of the spring semester. Kitty returned to boarding school in the fall, surviving only by imagining that she was protected by Mary Ann's spirit.

Throughout the rest of her life Kitty remained convinced that Mary Ann was always nearby looking after her. When her son, Roy, was born, she believed that Mary Ann was holding her hand during labor, and years later told Roy that they both had a guardian angel named Mary Ann Wilson who would protect them from harm.

One night not long after Kitty had her second stroke, Mary Ann appeared in Kitty's bedroom. Her hair was on fire. Tentacles of orange, red and yellow flames wriggled from her head.

MARY ANN'S HAIR
ON FIRE

"Mary Ann," Kitty whispered, "do you know that your hair is on fire?"

"It happens sometimes," said Mary Ann. "At first my mother was frightened but I wasn't. I knew the flames would not spread to others."

"But why does it happen? Isn't your scalp burning?"

"I don't feel the heat. The flames are God's fingers caressing me."

When Kitty was ninety-one years old, on her deathbed in a hospital, a nurse attending her told Roy that his mother believed a woman named Mary Ann was coming to take her away to a place where she would never again feel pain or be alone.

"I asked your mother if Mary Ann was very old and she said, 'Yes, she's thirteen, she'll be fourteen in June.'"

The Promise

The worst marriage Kitty made was her last. Her son, Roy, was gone by this time—"Out in the world somewhere" Kitty told people who asked her what he was doing. The most recent news she had from him was that he was working as a merchant seaman on freighters carrying cargo between Europe and South America. Her daughter, Sally, was nine years old, so she had no choice but to go along with Kitty's decisions regardless of how ill-conceived and self-destructive they might prove to be.

Kitty's fifth husband was Reno Mott. His first name was really Melvin but very early in their relationship Kitty could not remember it at a dinner party when she attempted to introduce him to friends of hers, so she said it was Reno, because that was where he was from. She thought it was funny and he did not seem to mind; thereafter, she called him Reno, as did Sally. He owned a box manufacturing company in Reno, Illinois, where he lived with his teenaged daughter from a previous marriage, to which town Kitty and Sally moved from Chicago. Kitty did not tell Roy about her latest marriage. She wrote to him irregularly in care of a friend of his in London, England, where Roy stayed when he was not at sea, and informed him only that she and his sister had moved to Reno, Illinois, ninety miles northwest of Chicago.

It was not long after their arrival in Reno before Kitty began to realize that the marriage had not been a good idea, especially for Sally. Reno Mott's daughter, Rowena, terrorized the younger girl. She resented Sally's presence and her mother's intrusion into Reno's and her life. Rowena did everything she could to make

Sally's existence there intolerable. No matter how Kitty attempted to ameliorate the situation, Rowena's cruelty toward her step-sister did not abate. In addition, her rudeness to and contempt for Kitty knew no limits. After six months Kitty told Mott that she and Sally were going back to Chicago. Reno Mott had made no attempt to mitigate his daughter's hostility. Whenever Kitty brought the matter up to him, he just shrugged and suggested that she ignore Rowena's nastiness, insisting that the girls would get along after they got to know each other better. This did not happen, so Rowena gladly agreed to leave and go to live with her mother, who also had remarried, in Akron, Ohio.

Rowena's departure improved daily life for Sally, but Kitty was disappointed by her husband's indifference to her complaints concerning financial matters—his box business was failing—and his refusal to properly include her in his social life, preferring to have Kitty stay at home with Sally while he went out with unidentified friends. This behavior did not sit well with Kitty. When she had met Mott in Chicago at a restaurant and agreed to have a date with him, he behaved graciously and was congenial to her friends. He told her then that he had a thriving business in Reno and that he was well-fixed for the future. "I'm a good catch for any woman," he said.

Kitty stuck it out for a year and was again on the verge of leaving Mott when he came home one day and declared that they were going to move to Phoenix, Arizona, where he had agreed to take a job as manager of a Ford dealership. The house in Reno was being foreclosed upon and the box business was bankrupt. They had no choice but to go.

Kitty told him that she had no intention of moving to Arizona, where she didn't know anybody, at which point Reno Mott became furious and left the house. That night, after getting drunk with a former girlfriend, Mott drove off a railroad bridge into a canal. The woman with him was pronounced dead at the scene from a broken neck, and Reno suffered two broken legs as well as a serious head injury that would most likely render him per-manently incapable of caring for himself. Kitty wanted nothing more to do with Reno Mott. She took Sally to Chicago, where she rented an apartment, got a job as a receptionist in a private hospital, and filed for a divorce.

When Roy arrived in Chicago, his mother told him what had happened. He asked her where Reno Mott was now.

"He's in a nursing home for disabled veterans in Reno," she said. "He was in the air force during the war. He's trying to get a government loan so he can afford to sue me for support. I'll never get married again, Roy, I promise."

Roy borrowed a friend's car and drove to Reno, Illinois, where he confronted Mott in the nursing home.

"If you don't leave my mother alone," Roy told him, "I'll kill you. Do you understand me?"

Kitty asked Roy if Reno Mott had said anything to him.

"Yes, he said he understood me and that I shouldn't worry because he had a job waiting for him in Phoenix and that as soon as he could walk again he was going there to sell cars."

Reno Mott

The Recital

The piano teacher, Bill, was a tall, slender man in his mid-thirties. He had wispy, thinning brown hair, and his concave posture gave those in his presence the unsettling feeling that his body could at any moment crumple into thirds. He wore wire-rim glasses and always spoke gently and encouragingly to Roy's daughter, Daisy, then eight years old, who was his student. Roy liked Bill. He told Roy that Daisy had some musical talent and it seemed to Roy that they genuinely enjoyed one another's company.

Bill did mention to Roy, however, that Daisy could be obstinate on occasion; that if she had a problem getting something right, even though he told her to let it go for the moment, that they could come back to it later, Daisy would often insist on working on the passage until she was at least satisfied with her progress. This kind of perseverance, Bill said, impressed him. He had seldom encountered a student so young who exhibited this degree of tenacity.

Daisy practiced less than she should have, Roy thought, but she said she liked taking piano lessons, so he did not mind paying for them even though it was an expense Roy barely could afford.

When it came time for her first recital, Daisy practiced the piece Bill had chosen for her to perform more diligently than usual. Roy noticed how her technique improved over the two or three weeks she rehearsed it. Bill mentioned to him how pleased he was by Daisy's dedication and on a Thursday after practice, two days prior to the recital, happily pronounced her performance-ready.

On Saturday Roy accompanied Daisy to Finnish Hall, a white

wooden building constructed at the turn of the century (the twentieth) by the Scandinavian community in their town. As the other participants, also accompanied by their family members and friends, filed into the hall, Roy noticed how many of the children—most well-dressed for the occasion—had worried expressions on their faces. Daisy, though she may also have been nervous, seemed calm.

The recital was organized according to age and skill levels. Daisy's group was to be last among five, and she had been scheduled seventh of the nine participants in her category. Finnish Hall was a pleasant venue in which to sit; the amber walls and hardwood flooring lent a soothing feeling to the proceedings. Daisy and Roy listened attentively to the other children as they played, and finally, after more than an hour, her turn came.

Daisy did not look at her father or at Bill before she stood and walked to the piano. A woman read aloud Daisy's name from a list, as she had for every child, and Daisy took her seat at the piano and began to play.

From the beginning Roy knew—and certainly Bill knew—that something was amiss. Daisy stumbled at the start, began again,

Daisy

continued to stumble but kept on despite hitting one wrong note or chord after another. When she finished, the audience applauded hesitantly and with considerably less enthusiasm than they had the efforts of the previous students. Either this child had a terrible case of nerves—in which case they might have been more generous in their response—or perhaps, the witnesses concluded, Daisy had simply not practiced properly and was ill-prepared for the event.

While Daisy played, Bill and Roy exchanged looks of puzzlement, and for good reason: she was attempting to play a piece other than the one she had so dedicatedly rehearsed. At the conclusion of her performance, Daisy immediately stood and walked back to her seat, took it, and stared straight ahead, not so much as glancing at Bill or Roy. Her father had seen that there were tears in her eyes, and he knew that she was struggling to hold them back. Roy said nothing to her while they sat and listened to the last two children play.

After the recital had concluded, Bill went over and sat next to Daisy. He asked her why she had not played the intended piece. There were still tears in Daisy's eyes, but Roy thought that she had fought past the urge to cry.

"Because three of the kids before me played it," Daisy told them, "I thought it would be better if I played a different one."

"But you hadn't practiced that piece," said Bill, very gently. "You weren't ready to play it."

Daisy sat for a moment without saying anything else, then she turned and looked at her father.

"I didn't want to be the same as everyone else," she said. "I'm sorry, Daddy."

Big tears rolled down her cheeks. Roy took her onto his lap and held her as she wept. Most of the other children and their families and friends had left the room.

Bill patted her softly on the back.

"You're a special person, Daisy," he said, "you really are."

"Come on, baby," Roy said to her, "let's get an ice cream."

Castor and Pollux in America

Roy met Trick Mullvaney in 1962, a couple of months after Trick got out of prison. Trick, whose Christian name was Patrick, was paroled to the custody of Roy's Uncle Buck, who provided him a construction job in Tampa, Florida, where Buck lived. Roy was fifteen at the time, Trick was twenty-two, the same age as Buck's son, Kip, who introduced them. Trick knew Kip from before he was sent to Raiford for stealing medical supplies—narcotics, mostly—from pharmacies in Hillsborough County. Kip persuaded his father to take a chance on Trick, which required Buck to sponsor and keep track of him for one year, the length of his parole. Roy's uncle rented an apartment for Trick on a property he owned near the construction site Trick worked on with Kip, building townhouses north of Tampa in Temple Terrace. Kip and Roy, when he was visiting from Chicago for the summer, lived with Buck and his wife, Belita, Kip's stepmother.

Trick took his wife, Lorelei, and their four-year-old daughter, Tanya, to live with him. Trick was good-looking, tall and lean, fair-haired, and had a Van Dyke beard he began growing as soon as he was released from "durance vile," as Buck referred to imprisonment. Roy's uncle had had a taste of it himself when he'd been in the marines, having spent four months in the brig for bringing girls into the barracks to service the men. He had been spared a dishonorable discharge thanks to his father bribing a congressman he had helped to get elected.

"Raiford isn't so bad," Trick told Kip and Roy, "compared to local and county lockups. Negroes do all the dirty work, of course, this being the South. Shouldn't be that way, but state prisons in the North aren't much different. They're segregated, too, even in New Hampshire, where I grew up."

The boys were sitting and drinking beer in Trick and Lorelei's living room after work. Roy was also on the job, shovelling lime rock off the curbs where Buck's construction company was paving streets.

"Can't be fun, huh, Roy?" Trick said. "Hundred and some out there every day, hotter when those trucks come through shootin' asphalt. How much is your uncle paying you?"

"A dollar an hour."

"Negroes get eighty-five cents," said Kip.

"It's not right," Lorelei said. "What if they have families? That's not a living wage."

Trick laughed. "In Raiford all the inmates get paid the same, nine cents an hour. Don't go to prison, Roy, no matter what state you're in."

"Roy won't never do a jolt," said Kip. "He's too smart, he'll go to college. Isn't that right, cousin?"

"I'm goin' to college after I'm off parole," said Trick, "then maybe divinity school. I got tight with a parson in Raiford. He'd had a good life, he told me, until he got caught puttin' it to an eleven-year-old girl. Couldn't keep his hands and other body parts off underage poontang. Roscoe Rainwater. There he was in a North Florida swamp with me layin' sewer pipe instead of little girls. Told me he quoted scripture all the while he was taking his pleasure."

"Quit, Patrick!" said Lorelei. "No more trashy jailhouse stories. I don't want Tanya to ever know you were in prison."

"You're right, honey, I've got to fight to keep my mind clean, but it's damn sure hard work."

"Do you like living in Chicago, Roy?" Lorelei asked. "What do your parents do?"

"My father's dead and my mother gets married."

"He was only five when his dad died," said Kip. "And his mother's been married three times since."

"Jesus on a pony," said Trick. "Ain't life grand?"

"It will be for Tanya," said Lorelei.

"I'll do my best to make that happen, darlin'," Trick said. "If I don't, promise you'll shoot me."

Lorelei looked directly into her husband's eyes when she said, "I promise."

Trick maintained his good behavior during the year he worked for Roy's uncle, and after his term of parole ended he passed a high school equivalency examination and enrolled in the University of South Florida in Tampa. He did passably well there and two years later entered the Pontius Pilate School of Divine Investigation in nearby Boca Lupo, from which he earned a certificate entitling him to call himself a Doctor of Divine Investigation and proselytize wheresoever God directed him to go.

Kip, meanwhile, had a falling out with his father over a navy insurance policy Kip wanted Buck to sign over to him and moved to Las Vegas, Nevada, where he became a card dealer. He worked there in various casinos for a few years but became an alcoholic. His alcoholism caused him to be fired repeatedly until he was no longer employable in Vegas. He bounced around the country, working as a taxi driver in Denver, an elevator operator in Chicago, a janitor in Kansas City, and a fruit picker in Texas.

During all of this time Kip and Trick Mullvaney stayed in touch by mail and occasional phone calls. Trick and Lorelei started a church in Boulder, Colorado, where they bought a big house on a mountainside with money Lorelei inherited from her parents following their deaths in an automobile accident. Tanya graduated from the University of Colorado with a degree in engineering, after which she moved to Montana.

Trick proved himself successful as a pastor but soon fell prey to what he referred to as Roscoe Rainwater Syndrome, which caused his downfall. After losing the majority of his parishioners, he began playing the stock market with the remainder of Lorelei's inheritance, eventually losing it all. Their house was foreclosed upon and his Church of Divine Wrath and Retribution was shuttered. Lorelei filed for divorce and went to live with Tanya in Montana, where Tanya worked as a civil engineer in the city of Bozeman. Lorelei never again spoke to Trick, shed the name Mullvaney, and soon remarried to a local real estate salesman named Ripley Palmer. Tanya refused to answer her father's letters or take his phone calls, ignoring his repeated requests that she send him money. She married a firefighter who threatened to murder Trick if he did not cease trying to contact Tanya.

Trick returned to Tampa, where, like Kip in Denver, he became a taxi driver. The Pontius Pilate School of Divine Investigation had closed due to its founder, Franklin Furto, having been convicted of defrauding several businessmen who had been on the school's board of directors. He was sentenced to serve fifteen years in the state prison at Raiford, which gave Trick a chuckle. Trick lost his looks and drank himself to death at the age of forty-two, not long before Kip, depressed and destitute, shot himself in the head while sitting on the steps of the entrance to a fast food restaurant in Phoenix, Arizona.

Roy, who never did go to college, nevertheless travelled the world and became a successful author of popular adventure novels for boys. He lived in Santa Fe, New Mexico, and corresponded frequently with his Uncle Buck, who informed Roy of Trick's early demise and his son Kip's suicide. Buck outlived both of them, passing away in his sleep at the age of ninety-three.

Roy was troubled and mystified by the facts of how his cousin Kip and Kip's pal Trick Mullvaney had led such pathetic lives and come to terrible, if not tragic, ends. When Roy was fifteen, they had been kind to him, generous with the little money they had, did their best to keep him out of trouble and harm's way, and always welcomed his company. Roy decided to write a novel about two young friends named Trick and Kip and their often humorous adventures and misadventures together. He would make everything up.

Trick Mullvaney

The Chinese Shadow

Roy's Uncle Buck Colby, his mother's brother, was a world trav- eller, and three weeks before his ninety-third birthday he decided to go to Havana, Cuba. He had two homes, one on Utila in the Bay Islands of Honduras, and the other in Tampa, Florida. He had been to Cuba many times, beginning in the 1940s, but not for several years; he was curious to see for himself how things had changed, if at all, since Fidel Castro had died.

Buck went by himself, he was fluent in Spanish and remem- bered his way around Havana. He stayed at the National, in its day the most elegant hotel on the island, now a bit run down, but still redolent of older, better times. He walked around the city, dallied as much as he was capable of dallying with a few of the plentiful array of prostitutes; went fishing out of Matanzas; played cards and gambled in the government owned casinos and in illegally operated bars in Havana viejo. After a week, however, he'd run out of things to do; without steady companionship, he was lonely and made arrangements to fly back to Tampa.

The day before he left, Buck encountered Hardy Farkas, an old acquaintance whom he had known since both of them had lived in Chicago more than half a century before. Buck had started his construction business and Farkas, who was twenty years younger, was a runner for Barney Rothman, an alderman on the west side. Buck asked him what he was doing in Havana.

"The girls, what else?" said Hardy. "I've still got somethin' left. I'm not seventy yet! You?"

"I don't know what I've got left."

Farkas laughed. "I bet the ladies know. I'm livin' in Miami now, in the jewelry business. Last I heard you were retired somewhere in the Caribbean."

"Honduras."

"What do you do there?"

"Fish, mostly. I live on an island."

"Got an island girl? I could come visit sometime."

"Life's pretty slow there."

"If you're in Miami, look me up. I've got a store in Coral Gables."

Buck remembered when Barney Rothman was shot and killed in a motel in Cicero with somebody's wife. The word was that he was set up by one of his own people, probably Farkas. After that, Hardy went to work for Gus Madigan's gang. You couldn't trust anybody in Chicago in those days.

Buck flew back to Tampa and as he was on an escalator headed down to the baggage claim, he was bumped into by another passenger in a hurry. Buck fell, injuring his head, back and legs. He was hospitalized and doctors told his daughter, Renalda, who also lived in Tampa, that he would most likely never walk again; also that her father's kidneys had failed, which would require treatment by dialysis. In addition, he may have incurred brain damage. His travelling days were over.

Renalda explained all of this to Buck as he drifted in and out of consciousness. On his third day in the hospital he told her that there was a Chinese shadow in his room, a veil covering his eyes. He was struggling, he said, to see through it.

"Your mother used to wear veils. Her eyes were a little crossed, she didn't like it when someone noticed. Where is she now?"

"In Madrid, she's remarried."

"I should go see her."

"Why Chinese?" Renalda asked. "Why a Chinese shadow?"

"On the Yangtze River, flowing from Kunlun Shan. I was sailing."

Buck tried to open his eyes but he could not.

"Let go, Colby," said Renalda.

When Renalda called Roy's mother, Kitty, who lived in Wisconsin, to tell her that Buck had died, Kitty said, "You know I'm fourteen years younger than my brother, I didn't see him very often, but I always enjoyed knowing that he was out somewhere in the world doing crazy things."

"You should go on thinking that way, Aunt Kitty, that he's still travelling."

"We all are, aren't we?"

After she hung up, Kitty repeated out loud, "Aren't we?"

"'Aren't we' what?" asked her daughter, Sally, who had just walked into the room.

"Travelling."

"You going somewhere?"

"No, Sally, not yet."

ROY'S UNCLE BUCK

Her Diary

Kitty had never kept a diary, even when she was a girl. Now that her son, Roy, was almost twelve, had a job and was in school most of the day, she had more time to herself. She was unmarried, for a change, and by choice or circumstance, she was not certain which, did not have a steady boyfriend. Her eczema was in a particularly virulent stage so she did not feel like socializing. Not only that, but her body ached constantly, something she had not experienced previously. Kitty was thirty-four years old and did not understand why she should be suffering this way. Other than prescribing ointments to treat the sores on her skin, the doctors Kitty consulted told her they were unable to identify more serious physical maladies, their consensus being that her problems were psychosomatic. Symptoms of an emotional disorder, a dermatologist said.

Kitty decided to keep a daily record of her condition, to write down in detail how she felt. Her ailments, Kitty was convinced, were in no ways imaginary. The pain was real and she needed to tell someone about it, even if the only person who believed her was herself. She bought a leatherbound diary and a good pen at a stationery store, walked to Indian Boundary Park and sat down on an unoccupied bench. It was a pleasant late spring day, one-thirty in the afternoon. Kitty opened the diary to the first page and wrote, "Why am I in so much pain?"

"Pardon me, ma'am. Are you all right?"

Kitty opened her eyes and saw a woman about her own age, perhaps a few years younger, standing in front of her. Holding the woman's right hand was a little boy who looked to be three or four years old.

"My goodness," said Kitty, sitting up straight, "I must have fallen asleep."

"Are these yours?" asked the woman, holding out to her both the diary and the pen with her free hand. "They were on the ground. You must have dropped them."

"Oh, thank you," Kitty said, and took them.

Kitty stood up but she was unsteady. The woman took hold of Kitty's right elbow and held it until Kitty could stand without wobbling.

"I'm so sorry to trouble you. I'd better go home and lie down. What a beautiful little boy. I have one myself. His name is Roy, he's older now."

"Do you live around here? We'd be happy to walk there with you."

"No, no, I'm all right now, I can navigate. My house is only a block away."

"My name is Marsha, and this is Steven."

"I'm Katherine. Kitty."

"I hope we meet again, Kitty, when you're feeling better."

"I do, too. Thanks again. And thank you, too, Steven."

Marsha and her son walked away. Steven turned to look back and waved. Kitty waved and smiled at him. She put the diary and pen into her purse, straightened her dress and pushed hair away from her eyes. Kitty took a few steps, then stopped and stood perfectly still. She felt a soft breeze. There was no pain.

Many years later, after his mother's death, Roy found Kitty's diary in one of her dresser drawers. He read the sentence on the first page, then leafed through the book. She had never written anything else.

The Pillow

Roy's father never complained. He knew he was dying from an incurable disease, that there was no recommended treatment other than the use of morphine when the pain became intolerable. After he was operated on unsuccessfully, Roy's father had to sit on a rubber pillow placed on a chair at the kitchen table. Roy, who was five years old, asked him if he could sit on it and his father said, "Sure, son, it's soft and bouncy."

Many years later, Roy thought about this moment and how hard his dad tried to not allow the illness to change the way he related to people, especially his son. Roy's father was forty-eight years old when he died. When he was told that his dad had passed away, Roy did not understand that death meant not only that he could not forget the final days of his father's life but that he would not want to.

1940

1956

Uncle Buck's Last Words

Roy's Uncle Buck was asleep in bed in a hospital. Roy sat on a chair next to the bed. Suddenly, Buck woke up and saw his nephew.

"Oh, Roy, I didn't know you were here."

"It's almost your birthday, Unk. You'll be ninety-three tomorrow."

"When was I born?"

"In 1911, in Chicago."

"I was dreaming that I was back in Africa, hiking alone through the bush. It must have been in Kenya, or maybe Tanzania. Yes, Tanzania, because Dar es Salaam was also in the dream. I had a small bag strapped over one shoulder, I'd packed a lunch. A native appeared and stood in front of me. He was very tall and half-naked. I greeted him in Swahili, 'Habari za asubuhi,' good morning, but he didn't reply. He stood still and stared down at me. I noticed that he had a knife stuck in his belt."

"What happened then?"

"I handed him my lunch."

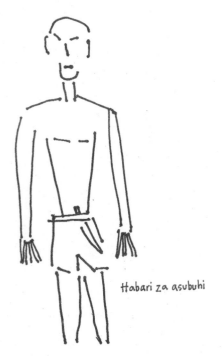

Habari za asubuhi

"He didn't say anything?"

"No, he took it and disappeared back into the bush."

Buck closed his eyes.

"So will I," he said.

La hombrada

She was with another man when Roy met her. Nothing unusual about that but she wouldn't look him in the eyes. She knew he was staring at her. She shook her long, tangled hair out of her river crocodile eyes but it didn't do the job. She didn't want to make it any easier for him. Was she introduced when they sat down at the table? Roy hadn't paid attention, only looked at her. She pretended that she did not understand English. Later in the evening a stranger at their table said something Roy didn't like so Roy called him a pendejo. The stranger pulled out a knife and a friend of Roy's took it away from him. Roy had stood up and was ready to fight but she spat at the man and called him a culero. On their way out of the bar she said to Roy, "Mexican men are cowards, that's why they carry knives and guns." They walked together on the pier, there was no moon. She took his hand and held it. Roy thanked her for sticking up for him. "De nada," she said. "I am Totonac, there are a few women in Mexico like me."

The Window

Walking alone in Paris on a rainy Sunday, Roy found himself on rue de l'Odeon in the sixth arrondissement in the early morning, only a couple of other solitary walkers on the street, men with berets pulled down over their foreheads. Roy stopped in front of a bookshop window. The year was 1965, he was eighteen years old, destitute and homeless. The night before, having fallen asleep on a bench in the Gare d'Austerlitz, he had been shaken awake by an attendant demanding that he show a ticket for a morning train. Only passengers with valid tickets were allowed to wait inside the station. Since Roy had no ticket to produce, he was ordered to leave. It was after midnight before he found shelter under a bridge among other bums who had sought a place to sleep. This was early October but the weather had already turned cold and now the rain had started. He settled into a vacant spot, separated by several feet from a dozen snoring men. Roy was one of them, les clochards, tramps, lost souls. There was nothing romantic about it. He needed to acquire enough money to take a train and then a ferry across the Channel back to England, to London, where he'd been living before taking off to explore the Continent. His friends there would help him out, at least give him a place to stay while he looked for work.

Roy paused to inspect the books displayed in the window. Being Sunday, the shop was closed. All of the titles were in French, as well as the literary magazines and journals. Several issues of the most prestigious journal, *La Nouvelle Revue Française*, or *NRF*, founded by André Gide in 1909, were given the most prominence.

There were photographs of contributors on the covers, as well as listings of their works contained in that particular issue. Among them were writers such as Sartre, Camus, Reverdy and Duras. Roy thought of himself as a writer, though he was as yet unpublished. He asked himself, "How do I get from where I am, an indigent vagabond on an unfamiliar street, to *there*, a person featured on the cover of *La Nouvelle Revue Française*?"

Twenty-five years later, Roy's name was on those covers, his stories, essays and poems contained in what would eventually become six issues of the *NRF*. *La Nouvelle Revue Française* ceased

LA NOUVELLE

REVUE FRANÇAISE

JANVIER 2010 – N° 592

DAVID BORATAV SIG-SAUER P226
CORINNE D'ALMEIDA AMOUR
PHILIPPE LE GUILLOU LE PIED ÉGYPTIEN
JEAN-PAUL MICHEL RIMBIENNES
BARRY GIFFORD TROIS RÉCITS
STÉPHANE AUDEGUY MEMORABILIA : LE GPS
JACQUES CHESSEX MARCEL ARLAND À MONTREUX

ALBERT CAMUS CORRESPONDANCE INÉDITE
AVEC MICHEL GALLIMARD

•

CRITIQUE

DONATIEN GRAU SITUATIONS DE LA CRITIQUE
JEAN-PIERRE FERRINI LE MIROIR DE LA FICTION,
OU LE PARADOXE DU ROMANCIER
CHRISTOPHE FIAT DE L'INFLUENCE D'ANDRÉ GIDE
SUR UNE POP LITTÉRATURE
JACQUES RÉDA VERS UNE «ALPHYSIQUE» ?

publication early in the following century. To have been among those contributors to the *NRF* gave Roy perhaps his greatest gratification, a fulfillment of what more than a quarter of a century before had been a kind of crazy dream. Given the circumstance of his initial recognition of the distance between that teenage boy standing in the rain on the rue de l'Odeon, gazing at what appeared to him evidence of an alien universe, how could it be otherwise? Publishing his work in *La Nouvelle Revue Française* had remained an enduring symbol of success, one that was and would be no matter of importance to anyone other than himself. Roy was still looking through the window.

Strange Cargo

Many readers of the Roy stories have asked what happened to Roy after his adolescence, the point at which the several hundred pages of stories involving him, his family and friends, stopped. *Strange Cargo* found Roy ten years later, a veteran of the Vietnam War, living in Bangkok, Thailand, with ex–air force buddy Vinnie D., his partner in an air freight company.

Captain Roy and Vinnie D. operated Strange Cargo Air Freight Company out of Bangkok for twenty-seven years. They were compelled to close down due to a combination of factors that included more technically up-to-date competition, difficulties caused by an endemic respiratory virus that impeded expeditious supply, closure of flight routes and an inevitable need to move on with the remainder of their lives.

After Roy and Vinnie D. dismantled and sold the holdings of Strange Cargo, they went back to the United States where they worked for a short time as helicopter pilots for the Bureau of Land Management in Colorado, Nevada, Wyoming and Utah, rounding up and aiding in the capture of wild horses. They quit once they discovered that instead of inoculating the horses against equine diseases and releasing them in a preserve where they could continue to roam free, as they had been informed would happen upon being hired, the BLM systematically destroyed the herds and sold their remains to pet food companies.

Vinnie D. returned to Asia and retired to a Buddhist monastery in Nepal and became a monk. Captain Roy bought a small ranch on the Star Route in Mendocino County, California. He wrote a series of novels based on his and Vinnie D.'s experiences during their years operating Strange Cargo that achieved a modest but profitable popularity, several of which were adapted as feature films. He did not marry and after Vinnie D. left for Nepal they never saw each other again.

CAPTAIN ROY